Christmas Outside Of Eden

By

Coningsby Dawson

CHRISTMAS OUTSIDE OF EDEN

I

This is the story the robins tell as they huddle beneath the holly on the Eve of Christmas. They have told it every Christmas Eve since the world started. They commenced telling it long before Christ was born, for their memory goes further back than men's. The Christmas which they celebrate began just outside of Eden, within sight of its gold-locked doors.

The robins have only two stories: one for Christmas and one for Easter. Their Easter story is quite different. It has to do with how they got the splash of red upon their breasts. It was when God's son was hanging on the cross. They wanted to do something to spare him. They were too weak to pull out the nails from his feet and hands; so they tore their little breasts in plucking the thorns one by one from the crown that had been set upon his forehead. Since then God has allowed their breasts to remain red as a remembrance of His gratitude.

But their Christmas story happened long before, when they weren't robin red-breasts but only robins. It is a merry, tender sort of story. They twitter it in a chuckling fashion to their children. If you prefer to hear it first-hand, creep out to the nearest holly-bush on almost any Christmas Eve when snow has made the night all pale and shadowy. If the robins have chosen your holly-bush as their rendezvous and you understand their language, you won't need to read what I have written. Like all true stories, it is much better told than read. It's the story of the first laugh that was ever heard in earth or heaven. To be enjoyed properly it needs the chuckling twitter of the grown-up robins and the squeaky interruptions of the baby birds asking questions. When they get terrifically excited, they jig up and down on the holly-branches and the frozen snow falls with a brittle clatter. Then the mother and father birds say, "Hush!" quite suddenly. No one speaks for a full five seconds. They huddle closer, listening and holding their breath. That's how the story ought to be heard, after night-fall on Christmas Eve, when behind darkened windows little boys and girls have gone to bed early, having hung up their very biggest stockings. Of course I can't tell it that way on paper, but I'll do my best to repeat the precise words in which the robins tell it.

<h1 style="text-align:center">II</h1>

It was very long ago at the beginning of all wonders. Sun, moon and stars were new; they wandered about in the clouds uncertainly, calling to one another like ships in a fog. It was the same on earth; neither trees, nor rivers, nor animals were quite sure why they had been created or what was expected of them. They were terribly afraid of doing wrong and they had good reason, for the Man and Woman had done wrong and had been locked out of Eden.

That had happened in April, when the world was three months old. Up to that time everything had gone very well. No one had known what fear was. No one had guessed that anything existed outside the walls of Eden or that there was such a thing as wrong-doing. Animals, trees and rivers had lived together with the Man and the Woman in the high-walled garden as a happy family. If they had wanted to know anything, they had asked the Man; he had always given them answers, even though he had to invent them. They had never dreamt of doubting him — not even the Woman. The reason for this had been God.

Every afternoon God had come stepping down from the sky to walk with the Man through the sun-spangled shadows of the grassy paths. They had heard the kindly rumble of His voice like distant thunder and the little tones of the Man as he asked his questions. At six o'clock regularly God had shaken hands with the Man and climbed leisurely back up the sky-blue stairs that led to Heaven. Because of this the Man had gained a reputation among the animals for being wise. They had thought of him as God's friend. He had given orders to everybody — even to the Woman; and everyone had been proud to obey him.

It had been in April the great change had occurred. There had been all kinds of rumours. The first that had been suspected had been when God had failed to come for His customary walk; the next had been when He had arrived with His face hidden in anger. The trees of Eden had bent and clashed as if a strong wind were blowing. Everything living that was not rooted, had run away to hide. Nevertheless, when God had called to the Man, they had tiptoed nearer to listen. The trouble had seemed to be about some fruit. God had told the Man that he must not pluck it; he had not only plucked it, but had eaten of it. So had the Woman. It had seemed a small matter to make such a fuss about. They had supposed that God's anger would soon blow over and that everything would be again as friendly as before.

And so everything might have been had it not been for the Man. Instead of saying he was sorry, he had started to argue and blame the Woman. At that God had refused to speak with him longer. He had ordered the Man and Woman and all the animals to leave Eden immediately. He had given them no time to pack. Lining them up like soldiers, He had numbered them to make certain that none were missing and then, with the Man and Woman leading, had marched them beyond the walls and locked the golden gates of Eden against them forever.

Since then all had been privation and confusion. The animals, from regarding the Man as their lord, had grown to despise him. They had blamed him for their misfortunes. They had told him that it was his fault that they had lost their happiness and that God walked the earth no more. The woman had told him so most particularly. Of all the created world only the dog and the robin had remained faithful to him. The dog slept across his feet at night to keep them warm and the robin sang to him each dawn that he should not lose courage.

III

Through the world's first summer things had not been so bad, though of course the wilderness that grew outside of Eden was not so comfortable as the garden they had lost. In the garden no one had needed to work: food had grown on the trees to one's hand and, because it was so sheltered, the weather had been always pleasant. It hadn't been necessary to wear clothing; it hadn't been necessary to build houses, for it had never rained. Birds hadn't troubled to make nests, nor rabbits to dig warrens. Everybody had felt perfectly safe to sleep out-of-doors, wherever he happened to find himself, without a thought of protection.

Here in the wilderness it was different. There were no paths. The jungle grew up tall and threatening. Thorns leant out to tear one's flesh. If it hadn't been for the elephant uprooting trees in his fits of temper, no one would have been able to travel anywhere. One by one the animals slunk away and began to lead their own lives independently, making lairs for themselves. Every day that went by they avoided the Man and Woman more and more. At first they used to peep out of the thicket to jeer at their helplessness; soon they learnt to disregard them as if they were not there. From having believed himself to be the wisest of living creatures the Man discovered himself to be the most incompetent. Often and often he would creep to the gold-locked gates and peer between the bars, hoping to see God walking there as formerly. But God walked no more. As He had climbed back into Heaven, He had destroyed the sky-blue stairs behind Him. There was no way in which the Man could reach Him to ask His advice or pardon.

But it was the Woman who caused the Man most unhappiness. It wasn't that she despised and blamed him. He'd grown used to that since leaving Eden. Everybody, except the dog and the robin, despised and blamed him. The Woman caused him unhappiness because she was unwell—really unwell; not just an upset stomach or a headache. In Eden she had always been strong and beautiful, like sunlight leaping on the smooth, green lawn—so white and pink and darting. Her long gold hair had swayed about her like a flame; her white arms had parted it as though she were a swimmer. Her eyes had been shy and merry from dawn to dusk. She had been a darling; never a cross word had she spoken. The furry creatures of the woods had been her playmates and the birds had perched upon her shoulders to sing their finest songs.

Now she was wan and thin as a withered branch. Like the elephant uprooting trees, she often lost her temper. Sometimes she was sorry for her crossness; more often she wasn't. When the Man offered her things to eat, no matter what trouble he'd taken to get them, she'd say she wasn't hungry. And yet he loved her none the less for her perverseness. He was so afraid.... He couldn't have told you of what he was afraid, for nobody had had time to die in the world as yet. He was filled with dread lest, like God, she might vanish and walk the earth no more. So he cudgelled his brains to find things to cure her. He invented wrong remedies, just as in Eden he had invented wrong answers to the animals' questions. He was never certain whether they would do her good or harm; but he always assured her gravely that, if she'd only try them, she'd feel instantly better. She never did; on the contrary she felt worse and worse. Perhaps the wilderness was the cause. Perhaps it was the forbidden fruit she had eaten. Perhaps it was a little of both, plus a touch of Eden-sickness. She had never known an hour's ill-health up to the moment when she had eaten the fruit and been turned out of the garden. The poor Man was distracted. He didn't care what he did or whom he robbed, if only he might hear her singing again and see her once more smiling.

What he did wasn't tactful; it only made the animals hate him—all except the dog and the robin—and brought new dangers about his head. It was the month of October and nights were getting shivery. He had scraped together fallen leaves to make a bed for her and had woven a covering of withered grasses. In spite of this, from the setting of the sun till long after its rising, all through the dark hours her teeth chattered. She cried continually; every time she cried, out in the jungle the hyena scoffed. The Man rarely got any rest until full day. All night he was rubbing her back, her feet and hands in an effort to make her warm. As a consequence he slept late and accomplished hardly any work. He didn't even have time to notice how all the animals were building houses. The Woman was so fretful that he never dared leave her for longer than an hour. The poor thing was forever complaining that God might have made her out of something better than a rib, if He was going to make her at all.

It was a colder night than usual, when the Woman was crying very bitterly and the hyena was doing more than his ordinary share of scoffing, that the idea occurred to the Man. The hyena was scoffing because he was comfortable; he was comfortable because of the heavy coat that he wore. The Man determined to teach him a lesson by taking his coat from him. It was another remedy; he hoped that if he clothed the Woman with it, she might grow strong. Telling her that he wouldn't be gone for long, he padded stealthily away, followed by the dog, and faded out of sight among the shadows.

They found the hyena in an open space which the elephant had been clearing the day before. He was seated on his hind legs, gazing up at the moon with his fine warm coat all bristly, scoffing and scoffing. He was far too busy with his ill-natured merriment to hear them coming. In a flash the dog had him by the throat, holding him while the man robbed him of his clothing. When they had stripped him of everything, even of his bushy tail, they let him go and he fled naked, howling the alarm through the forest. By the time they got back to the Woman all the underbrush was stirring. From every part of the wilderness, in twos and threes, the animals were coming together. The night was alive with their glowing eyes; the leaves trembled with their savage muttering.

"Be quick," whispered the Man. "Put this on."

She dried her tears as she felt the warmth of the fur. "It's comfy," she sobbed. "It fits exactly." And then, "Oh, Man, I'm frightened. What have you done? You gave me a present once before."

The Man was making a club out of a tree. As he stripped it of its branches, he answered boastfully, "It was I and the dog; we did it together. You were cold, so we stole the hyena's coat from him. All the animals are angry. They know that we shall do again what we have done once. They feel safe no longer. They say it must be stopped. They want to get back the hyena's coat from us."

"And they will, oh, my master," the dog interrupted, "unless we protect ourselves. Through the wilderness, not many miles from here, a limestone ridge rises above the forest. In the limestone ridge there is a cave. If we can win our way to it before our enemies come together, we can stand in the entrance and guard the Woman."

So the dog ran ahead growling with such fierceness that everything fled from his path. Behind him came the Man carrying the Woman very closely because he loved her, and trailing his tremendous club. By dawn, before their enemies could guess their purpose, they had gained the cave. By the time the animals had held their conference and decreed that the Man and the dog must be punished, they had escaped and were ready to defy all comers.

IV

From that moment a new and exciting kind of life started. Not an hour out of the twenty-four was free from anxiety. Always, whether it was day or night, the Man and the dog had to take turns at guarding the entrance. The Man gathered piles of stones and learnt how to throw them unerringly. The dog trusted to his teeth and the fear which his bark inspired. The animals were furiously determined; they never ceased from attempting to surprise them. Quite often they would have succeeded, had it not been for the robin, who hiding in the bushes, overheard their strategies and flew back to the Man in time with warnings.

The cave was well chosen. It was approached by a steep and narrow path. Only one enemy could attack at once, so the defenders were always able to roll down bowlders on him before he gained a footing. That was how they treated the lion, when he came thrashing his tail and roaring on the first morning to make them prisoners. They gave a rock a big shove and knocked him over like a ninepin. He was so hurt in his feelings that he sulked in bed for a week; for many more weeks he was easily tired. Seeing that he was the King of the Beasts and the President of their Conference, this made the animals the more indignant and the more determined that the Man and the dog must be punished. The next to attempt their capture were the elephant and the rhinoceros. They boasted that they weren't afraid of rocks; nevertheless they came together to back up each other's courage. Half way up the slope they stuck. They were too heavy for so steep a path. The ground crumbled from under them, the dog worried them, the Man struck them, and away they went, bumping down the hill, rolling over and over. They never stopped till they had reached the bottom, where they lay on their backs with their feet in the air, grunting and panting like a pair of upturned locomotives.

At first the Man and the dog regarded the enmity they had aroused in the light of a huge joke; they got a good deal of fun out of fighting. But the sporting side of the affair ceased to appeal to them when they were compelled to recognize the seriousness of their predicament. They were absolutely cut off from supplies at a season when food was running short.

They had to sneak out at night at the risk of capture to get anything to eat at all. They had a sick woman on their hands who cried not for food, but for delicacies. Instead of gathering strength, she grew steadily weaker. And then there was the matter of sleep; it was as scarce as food. They hardly snatched a wink of it. When they weren't on guard or fighting, they were soothing her fretfulness, foraging for her or thinking up some new method of keeping her warm. It was damp in the cave; sunlight rarely tiptoed farther than the entrance. It didn't take them long to discover that the hyena's coat had been as dearly purchased as the forbidden fruit that had lost them the garden. Peace, which they might have concluded in the early days, was now entirely out of the question. Even an offer to return the hyena's coat wouldn't have made any impression. They had carried hostilities too far; there wasn't an animal whom they had not wounded and who wasn't mad with them clean through from the point of his nose to the tip of his tail. Often and often, standing in the entrance to his cave, the Man would gaze longingly across the bronzy roof of the forest to the distant shining of the padlocked gates of Eden. He was farther than ever from the garden now with its tranquil blessedness. If only he hadn't learnt to steal! Stealing had been the cause of his downfall—first the forbidden fruit and then the hyena's coat. If he had been less enterprising and more obedient, he would still have been the friend of God. After a wakeful night he crept to the entrance to discover that the worst thing of all had happened.

"A worse thing!" you exclaim. "I thought you were going to tell us a cheerful Christmas story."

And so I am: but all the unfortunate part comes first—that's the way the robins tell it. If you'll be patient and read on, you'll find this is the very cheerfullest story that was ever told in earth or heaven. You may not have noticed that we've not yet come to the first laugh. The Woman has smiled and the hyena has scoffed; but no one has laughed. It's when we come to the first laugh that the happiness commences.

V

The worst thing of all that the Man discovered when he crept to the cave-entrance after a wakeful night, was this: with a terrible stealthy silence snow was drifting down so that even the distant shining of the gates of Eden was blotted out. It was frightening; snow had never fallen in the world before. If it had, the Man had not seen it. Within the walls of the garden summer had been perpetual. He stood there staring out forlornly at the misty sea of shifting whiteness. It chilled him to the bone. It seemed to him that the pillars of the sky had collapsed and the dust of the moon and stars was falling. Soon everything would be buried and the world itself would be no more. He looked at the calendar which he had scratched upon the wall. It was the twenty-fourth day of December. He wondered whether God knew what was happening and whether He had planned it. Then he gave up wondering, for behind him, from the blackness of the cave, the Woman called.

"Oh, Man," she cried, "I cannot bear this any longer!"

He groped his way to her and raised her in his arms so that her head lay on his breast. Even in the darkness he could see the glow of her hair, like the shadow of flame growing fainter and fainter.

"My Woman," he whispered, "what can I do for you?" And again he whispered, "What can I do for you?"

She pressed her face close to his before she answered, petting him the way she had been used to do in Eden. "Do for me? Nothing. You've tried with your remedies—you've tried so hard. Poor you! If we could only find God——"

"If we could," the Man said, "but——"

And then they both grew silent, for how could they find God when He had climbed back to Heaven, destroying the sky-blue stairs behind Him?

"Perhaps, He still walks in Eden." It was the Woman who had spoken. "If you were to go and watch through the bars of Eden till He comes and were to call to Him—if you were to tell Him that I cannot bear it any longer and that we're sorry, so sorry — that we did it in our ignorance — —" Without ending what she was saying, she fell to sobbing.

He didn't dare to tell her that the moon and stars were falling and that the gates of Eden were blotted out. From where she lay in the blackness of the cave she could see nothing; she was too weak even to crawl to the entrance. As he did his best to comfort her, "If we could only again find God — —" she kept whispering.

So at last, having ordered the dog to guard her, the Man departed on his hopeless errand. It was brave of him. He believed that in trying to find God, he would get so lost that he would never be able to retrace his footsteps. Before he went he kissed the Woman tenderly, begging forgiveness for all the misery he had caused her.

"But I caused it, too," she confessed. "It wasn't your rib that was to blame. It wasn't you at all. I wanted the fruit and we ate it together."

It was the first time she had acknowledged it; until then she had insisted that the fault was his solely. So in the moment of farewell she restored to him one little ray of the great, lost sun of flaming happiness.

VI

The air was so thick with falling snow that he was well-nigh stifled. His eyes were blinded as though they were padded with cottonwool. The flakes brushed against his cheeks like live things. At his sixth step from the entrance he had lost his direction. His feet commenced to slide; against his will he went avalanching and cavorting down the path.

At the bottom he lay panting for a time; then, because he was cold he picked himself up and went blundering on, not in the least knowing where he was going. Bushes clutched at his feet. Trees slashed across his face. He was inclined to weep, but checked himself, remembering that on one of those sunny afternoon walks God had told him that to cry wasn't manly. "And I must find God. I must find God," he kept repeating to himself. The only way he knew of finding God was by pressing forward. God had once confessed to him, "The reason I am God is because I show courage."

"Then I'll show courage, too," he thought.

Presently he found himself in the heart of the forest and began to breathe more freely. Avenues of giant trees stretched before him, which criss-crossed one another and faded into the gloom of twilit, colonnaded tunnels. He could almost feel the gnarled trunks bracing themselves and the crooked branches linking arms to bear up the weight of the down-poured roof of whiteness. As his eyes grew accustomed to the dimness, he saw the animals strewn flat among fallen leaves, their noses pressed between their paws, shivering with terror. Overhead birds and monkeys sat in rows, squeezed side by side for companionship, weeping silently. Of a sudden he regained his majesty, being filled with contempt for their cowardice. "For I am Man," he reminded himself, "so like to God that I could easily be mistaken for Him—and these are the creatures who dared to talk of punishing me."

Throwing out his chest, he strode valiantly past them, utterly ignoring their presence.

From behind him a voice called whimperingly. It was the lion's, the King of Beasts, squeaky and falsetto with panic. "Master, thou art wise. What has happened? Tell us."

Had he known how, the Man would have laughed. But the laugh comes later in the story. Without turning his head, still going away from them he answered. "It is a punishment for what thou and thy people have done to me and my Woman, oh, lion."

He had made the answer up on the spur of the moment; he knew no more than they did what had happened. But he loved inventing and was never so content as when he was pretending that he was God.

Immediately they forgot the wrong answers he had given them and how he had deceived them in the past. The leaves rustled as they lifted up their heads from between their paws. Their voices trembled as one when they besought him, "Master, stay with us. We are in terror. Make it leave off."

Turning slowly, he blinked at them through the dimness. Folding his arms, he regarded them thoughtfully with his legs wide apart. He did it as he supposed God might have done it. He spoke at last. "It's only just begun. Why should I make it leave off?"

"Because thou art strong and we are repentant."

Their manner was so humble and adoring that he felt sorry for them. They had begged his pardon in the same words that he had intended to beg God's. And then he was just—the only just creature that God had created. In his heart he knew that he had merited their revenge—there was scarcely one of them at whom he had not hurled his rocks. He came back walking in stately fashion till he stood fearlessly in the centre of them. Looking up through the burdened branches at the calamity which he did not understand, he commanded, "Leave off."

To his immense surprise, on the instant the snow ceased falling. It settled gently like a tired bird into its nest. The serenity of the stillness was unbroken.

"I am hungry," he said.

The animals hurried to their stores of food and waited on him.

"I have not slept."

The squirrels scraped fallen leaves into a bed, and the bear and the wolf stood guard.

When he awoke it was a brilliant winter's morning. The sun was charioteering in highest heaven. The forest was white as though cotton-wool had blown through it. As far as eye could search, everything glittered, sheathed in a film of glass. Snow bulged from branches like pillows filled to bursting. Icicles hung down like fantastic swords. Down the colonnaded avenues trees cast their shadows in heavy bars; the spaces between them were golden splashes.

The Man yawned. "I am still tired. Fetch the horse that he may carry me back to my dwelling."

He ordered the horse to be fetched because he had forgotten where his cave was. It was clever of him. He did it to keep the animals from knowing his ignorance.

The horse came galloping up obediently. Clutching him by the mane, the Man bestrode him. Off they started at a sharp trot, with the animals shouting and bounding beside them. As they travelled, the Man could hardly keep from smiling at picturing what a fine fellow he was. He made no attempt to restrain himself from giving orders. All the time he kept urging the animals to shout louder. He wanted the Woman to hear them, so that she might crawl to the entrance of the cave and be a witness of his triumphant home-coming. It wasn't good enough merely to picture himself as a fine fellow. He was anxious to hear her say to him, "Oh, Man, what a fine fellow you are!" He'd forgotten completely the purpose of his errand — that he'd set out through the world's first snowstorm in search of God.

So at last they burst forth from the forest and reached the foot of the slippery ascent. Because it was so slippery, the Man dismounted; the horse could carry him no further. Having commanded the animals to go on shouting for at least half-an-hour, he left them and commenced to climb the steep and narrow path. He had to go gingerly on his hands and knees.

There were places where he slipped back two steps for every one he advanced. By snatching at rocks and bushes, he dragged himself slowly to the turning which brought him in sight of the entrance. There, seated in the entrance to the cave, he saw ...

You must remember that by now it was the twenty-fifth of December. To remember that is most extraordinarily important. What he saw is so exciting that it deserves another chapter.

VII

He saw the Woman — but not the Woman as he had left her. She was no longer sick. She was completely restored. As in the old days her hair clothed her like a flame. Her face parted it into waves as though she were a swimmer. He could see the pink dimples in her knees where she sat and the marble whiteness of her feet, which flashed like jewels. She was again the darling who had delighted his heart when she had darted like a sunbeam across the shaven lawns of Eden; but now she was ten times more radiant.

What was it that had changed her? Her tenderness made a golden mist about her which inspired him with awe. He had had precisely this sense of sunny quietness when he had walked through those long, still afternoons with God.

She was unaware of him. Her eyes were deep pools of sapphire. She was smiling gently and brooding above something which nestled in her arms. He called to her softly; she paid him no attention. Far below the ridge, in obedience to his commands, the animals were still shouting. Was it because of them that she was smiling? Had the robin flown ahead of him to tell her what had happened? The robin was perched on her shoulder, fluttering his little wings and singing her his finest song. He called to the robin; like the Woman, the robin was too occupied to hear him. No, it wasn't because of him that she was smiling — he felt sure. Then why was it?

He gazed back on the dazzling landscape that spread away below him, hoping to find something there that would tell him. How transformed it was from the gloomy jungle that had been wont to threaten him! It was like a nest of down. From its farthest edge where Eden lay, a beam of glory spanned it with an orange path. It was this beam that made the golden mist about the Woman. To his amazement he saw that Eden's gates were open. Even while he watched they began to close, slowly and slowly, with the beam ever shortening, till at last they were utterly locked and barred.

The memory of lost happiness overwhelmed him. He turned again to the Woman. There she sat in the golden mantle of her hair, enthroned on the snow's pure whiteness. Creeping to her humbly, he fell to covering her feet with kisses, so great was his need of her.

"My Woman," he wept, "they are cold—so cold. Never again will I leave thee, not even to find God."

She bent towards him, lifting his chin in her hand. "I shall feel the cold no more. Put thy hand in my breast. Dost thou feel it? I have that next my heart which, though I grow old, shall keep me forever warm."

As he slipped his hand in her breast, she parted her hair and showed him. Kneeling beside her, he gazed down wonderingly at a thing that he had never seen before. He could find no name for it. It was like himself and it was like her also, only it was tiny and no thicker than his fore-arm. It had wee feet and hands, a rose-bud of a mouth and it was smooth and soft. Its head, which was the size of an apple, was covered with silky floss. Lowering his face, he sniffed it all over. It smelt sweet like the flowers that used to bloom in Eden.

"What is it?"

She shook her head. "It was here when I wakened." Her eyes became bright and immense as stars. "It's our's," she whispered tenderly.

VIII

It was awkward to have something for which you could find no name, especially when it was something that you had begun to love already.

"We'll have to ask someone," the Man said. "If I knew where He was, I might ask——"

The Woman's face blanched. "Not God," she begged. "Because of the fruit we ate, He might take it from us."

Just then they were disturbed by a rustling of snow. Looking up, they saw the rabbit, watching them with timid eyes and recovering his breath after the long climb.

"What d'you want?" the Man asked sharply.

The rabbit flicked his white scut and sat up on his hind-legs, his whiskers quivering with excitement.

"I want to see it," he panted. "The dog's been boasting. I hurried because I wanted to be the first to see it. I'm so little; I couldn't do it any harm."

"Let him see it," said the Woman. "He's gentle. He might be able to tell us what to call it."

So the Man told the rabbit that he could have just one peep. But when the rabbit tried to get his peep by standing against the Woman's knees, he wasn't tall enough, so the Man had to lift him till he lay all furry against the little creature that was in the Woman's arms.

"I can't suggest anything," said the rabbit. "We ought to consult the other animals. They all want to be friends; they're so curious. But there's one thing I do know: we're both small and my coat would just fit it."

Before they could stop him, he had pulled off his coat and was tucking it snugly about the little stranger. He was right; it did fit exactly. So the first garment of the earth's first baby was a rabbitskin, which accounts for the rhyme which mothers sing about "Gone to fetch a rabbitskin, to wrap the baby bunting in."

When the rabbit had presented his gift, he hopped down from the Woman's lap very much thinner.

"And now can I bring the other animals?" he asked.

The Man hesitated. He was remembering the last visits of the lion and the elephant and the rhinoceros. "They might find a name for it," the rabbit pleaded.

Then the Man nodded and the rabbit scuttled off.

They hadn't long to wait before they heard a deep breathing and grunting. Struggling up the frozen path to the cave came all the animals that God had created. They advanced in single file, the great and the small mixed up together; the giraffe followed by the hedgehog and the mastodon preceded by the frog. They came hand-in-hand, forming a chain to pull one another up, treading on each other's heels, jostling and slipping back on one another. Those behind kept whispering to those in front to hurry; those in front were too winded to retort. Their ascent was made more difficult by their generosity, for all save one of them carried presents. The one who came empty-handed was the stork. He led the procession looking stately and pompous, as though he were taking the credit for having occasioned the disturbance. The Man learnt later that that was precisely what he was doing—taking all the credit. He had been telling the animals that it was he who had left the strange little creature at the Woman's side the night before. Because of this he pretended that it wasn't necessary for him to bring a present. There were many who believed him. There still are.

When they had all climbed safely to the top they gathered in a semi-circle about the Woman, having piled their gifts before her. In silence they waited; then she parted her hair and showed them the wonder that nestled in her arms.

The Man, standing at her side, addressed them. "Oh, brothers, I am wise, for I have walked with God; yet have I never seen anything like it. There was nothing like it in Eden. I have sent for you that I may ask you what to call it."

No one answered. He questioned each in turn, but none of them could advise him.

"We have to find a name for it," he said crossly; "so let's sit down and think hard."

So they sat down in the snow, scratching their heads, and thought hard. From time to time the Man enquired whether any of them had had an inspiration. They never had, which was discouraging when you consider what a lot of them were thinking. In this way at least an hour must have passed.

Things were getting both cold and embarrassing, when the little creature, who was being thought about so hard, showed signs of waking and began to stir in the Woman's arms. I ought to have told you that ever since the Man's home-coming it had been sleeping. First it kicked out with its bandy legs. Then it fisted its pudgy hands and yawned. Then it puckered its wee red face in a manner most alarming and, to the amazement of them all.... The Woman was so amazed that she nearly let it drop. And yet what it did was perfectly natural; it opened its eyes, like two blue patches of heaven, and blinked at them. Last of all it emitted a thin, wailing sound that made everybody abominably unhappy. The crocodile became so emotional that his tears froze in two long icicles. After a pause the sound was repeated. All the animals rose on their hind-legs and covered their ears with their paws.

The Woman stared at them apologetically. She was distressed and puzzled. "Please don't cover your ears," she begged. "And don't think that I'm hurting it. There's something that it's trying to tell us. It's said the same thing before. It began saying it the moment I first found it. It's gone on saying it, on and on.... There, there my little one, my belovedest."

As if to corroborate her assertion that it had gone on and on, it commenced to cry afresh. Out of politeness to the Woman, though the sound hurt them, the tenderhearted animals uncovered their ears and listened intently. This is what they heard, repeated over and over, "Baa-aa-by! Baa-aa-by! Baa-aa-by!"

They were all shaking with sobbing when the elephant, in his coarsest manner, lifted, up his trunk and snorted through it contemptuously.

"Stop snorting," the Man ordered impatiently. "There's no reason why you should snort."

"Isn't there?" The elephant shuffled to his feet to depart. Before he went, just to show his independence, again he snorted. Across his shoulder he remarked. "And you think yourself so wise! You want to know what to call it. Every time it speaks it tells you." It cried once more. "There you are!" The elephant trumpeted triumphantly as he seated himself at the top of the slide, having pulled his tail from under him preparatory to tobogganning down the path. "Don't you hear what it says? 'Baa-aa-by! Baa-aa-by!' It couldn't be put more plainly. It's asking you to call it baby."

As the elephant pushed off and vanished in a whirl of flying snow, the Woman turned to the Man with a smile of gladness. "The clumsy fellow's right. Weren't we the stupids? Fancy not understanding our own baby!"

IX

As you may imagine, all the beasts and birds went back to the jungle very discontented. They didn't see why they shouldn't have babies. They were wild to have babies. They talked of nothing else. No sooner had they got down the hill from visiting the cave than they turned round and started to climb back again. They kept urging the Woman to be frank with them and to confess how her baby had happened. Of course she couldn't confess, seeing that she didn't know herself. All that she knew was that she hadn't felt well since she had eaten the forbidden fruit in Eden and, now that the baby had been born, she felt completely restored. Such information wasn't of much use to the animals, for the forbidden fruit grew inside of Eden and the gates of Eden were locked. At last the Man had to interfere to prevent her from being bothered. He stuck up a notice at the entrance to the cave, December 25th. Mother And Child Both Doing Well. Don't knock. When the animals came to call, he prevented them from entering by explaining gravely that having a baby was a very touch-and-go business and left one decidedly exhausted. To have listened to him you might have supposed that he'd spent all his life in rocking cradles, whereas he was such a novice that, had it not been for the elephant, he wouldn't even have known that babies were called babies. Like all fathers he deceived himself that there was nothing he didn't know about baby-lore. What was very much more surprising, by whispering and looking secretive he managed to impress the animals with his new-found learning and paternal importance.

But what had happened to the robin while all these excitements were going on? The last time we mentioned him he was sitting perched on the Woman's shoulder, singing her his very finest song.

The robin, though you may not have heard it, has always been a most religious bird. He had made up his mind, the moment the Man had come back, that the first thing to be done was to go and tell God. The chief difficulty about accomplishing this errand was due to God Himself; as you will remember, in returning to Heaven God had destroyed the sky-blue stairs behind Him. But the robin had wings; moreover he was an optimist. He hoped that by fluttering up and up he would be able to reach Heaven in safety. The reason that he had never tried before was because he had been afraid that God would not want him. He felt sure of his welcome now that he was the bearer of such glad tidings.

He found the journey much harder than he had expected. There were parts of it that were so bitter that his wings would scarcely flutter. After he had lost sight of earth, he had to wind his way between the burning stars; they were so close together in places that his feathers were scorched. But he pressed on valiantly till he made out the quiet shining of the gates of Heaven and entered through the unguarded walls of jasper into a garden, which was in no way different from the one that God had planted upon earth.

Beneath scented trees the angels were scattered about disconsolately. There were black rims under their eyes; it was easy to see they had been worrying. Their beautiful white gowns had come unstarched; it was many days since they had tidied themselves. There wasn't a sound of any sort—least of all of music. Some of them still carried their harps; but most of them had stacked them in open spaces the way soldiers stack their rifles. When the robin sank spent to the grass in front of them, they paid him scant attention. When he weakly chirped his question, "Where's God?" they jerked their thumbs, indicating the direction, too listless to waste breath on words.

"What's the matter?" asked the robin.

"We're unhappy." After they had said it, they had difficulty to choke back their sobs.

"But why are you unhappy? Whoever heard of being unhappy in Heaven!"

"Because—because——." They glanced at one another forlornly, hoping that someone else would be the first to answer. "Because of the forbidden fruit. It's made God cross."

"Pshaw!" The robin swelled out his little breast with importance. "You'd better visit earth and see our baby. If the Woman hadn't eaten the forbidden fruit, there wouldn't be any baby."

The word "baby" was entirely new to them. They sat up beneath their scented trees and began to ask questions. But the robin didn't want to be delayed; he spread his wings and fluttered on.

At last he came to the smoothest of smooth lawns, in the midst of which grew a mulberry-tree, beneath whose shadow God was seated with the Virgin Mary. Despite the flakes of sunlight falling and the gold-blue peace by which They were surrounded. Their attitudes were no less despondent than the angels'. God sat with His elbows digging into His knees. His face was buried in His delicate hands. His eyes, peering through His fingers, were strained and red with always staring broodingly straight before Him. Of the Virgin Mary, crouching at His feet, the robin could only see the glint of her flaxen hair and the paleness of her narrow shoulders. Her head was bowed in the lap of her Maker as if she had been beseeching Him always.

The robin was overwhelmed with terror. All his chirpiness was gone. "Dear God," he quavered, "I beg Thy forgiveness. I have come when I was not bidden."

He paused, hoping that God would encourage him. When God took no notice, he felt himself to be the most insignificant and impertinent of living creatures. He spoke again, lest the silence should kill him on the spot.

"I have brought glad tidings—at least, we on earth think they are glad. The Woman, whom Thou didst cast out for eating the fruit that was forbidden, has been very sick. She has been sick since April till just before day-break this morning, when she miraculously recovered. At her side she found lying a little thing—such a little thing—so like to Thyself, oh, God. It has bandy legs and arms no thicker than Thy smallest finger. It has a baldy head, about the size of an apple, with threads of gold spread over it like floss. It has a pink, wee face and a rose-bud of a mouth. It's eyes are like patches of Thine own blue Heaven. And it's soft and cuddly. The Women calls it her 'Belovedest.' And it smells sweet like the flowers we used to breathe in Eden. We didn't know what it was. Even the Man didn't know. He summoned the animals to come and find a name for it. While they were sitting on their hind-legs, behold, it awoke and told us that its rightful name was baby. And now, oh, God, we birds and animals want to have babies. We're all trying to find out how it happened. And I want to find out most especially, because ——"

"A baby, thou sayest! What is a baby? I, thy Creator, know nothing of it. The last thing I fashioned was the Woman, who has brought this deep shame upon Us."

God had spoken through His hands very softly, yet His voice was like a great wind blowing. It took the robin some seconds to recover from the shock. By the time he was ready to answer, the angels were rustling through all the glades of Heaven and the Virgin was gazing at him with wistful intensity.

"What is a baby!" he said audaciously repeating God's words. "It is a little Man and a little God. Surely, Thou knowest?"

"I know nothing," God thundered, letting fall His hands from before His face. "Be gone."

When the hurricane of sound had ended, the robin found himself hovering in the gateway between the jasper walls, where the sheer drop which lies between earth and Heaven commences. He turned to look back before he took the leap and saw that behind him the angels were following. Following most closely was the Virgin.

"Tell me again," she pleaded. "It's little and soft. It's cuddly and it smells like the flowers that bloom in Eden."

Perched on her shoulder, with his beak against her ear, he twittered to her his tale once more. While he was telling her, the angels crowded round, smoothing his feathers with shy caresses. But he didn't dare to stay too long, for distantly from beneath the mulberry tree, he still felt the brooding eyes of God. Launching himself from the Virgin's shoulder, he sank between the burning stars and through the bitter coldness of clouds snow-laden, till late in the wintry afternoon he reached the cave on the limestone ridge, whence a murmur of secret singing was emerging.

X

On the threshold he paused to listen. Yes, it was the Woman. It was the first time she had been happy enough to sing since she had been cast out of Eden. But her song was entirely different from anything that she had sung before. It was more little and tender. It was a lullaby of mother-nonsense, which she hummed when she couldn't find the proper rhymes and made up as she went along.

As the robin fluttered through the gloom to her shoulder, she pressed her finger to her lips to warn him. The baby eyes were the merest slits of blueness. The little thumb was in the mouth and the baby lips were sucking hard. The tiny knees were digging into the Woman's body and the baldy head was cushioned on her bosom. The dog snoozed across her feet. The Man crouched against her, shrouded in the mantle of her hair, overcome with weariness. She was mothering them all, rocking herself slowly and singing gently her silly little song. The crooning of it over and over seemed to hush them with a sense of security.

"You are my ownty,

Dear little donty,

Sweetest and wonty,

Pudding and pie;

Good little laddie,

Just like your daddie.

Fallen from Heaven,

Come from the sky."

"But he didn't," whispered the robin.

The Woman paused in her singing. "Didn't what?"

"He didn't fall from Heaven. God's just been telling me; He never heard about him."

The Woman smiled. "Never heard about him! It doesn't matter; his Mummy's heard about him." She stooped to kiss the soft little bundle, for he had commenced to stir. Then she resumed her singing.

Gradually the day failed. The late afternoon faded into evening. Gray twilight stole swiftly down. For a while the white fields of snow outside reflected a vague dimness; then night came with a noiseless rush, closing up the entrance to the cave with a wall of blackness.

Perched on the Woman's shoulder the robin dozed. She still went on singing. How long he had been dozing he had no means of telling. He was wakened by a multitudinous rustling, as of a crowd assembling and drawing nearer. At first he thought that it was some of the more persistent of the animals, coming once more to urge the Woman to tell them how babies happened. Then, of a sudden, he knew that he had been mistaken. The gloom of the cave was lit up by a glowing brightness. Peering across the threshold, with all the haloed hosts of Heaven tiptoeing behind her, was the Virgin Mary. It was the crowd of haloes that was causing so much brightness.

Stepping to the Woman's side, she gazed down longingly at the small God-Man.

"I want one. Oh, I want one so badly," she murmured.

The angels, thronging behind her, folded their wings and repeated her words, "So badly! So badly!" The sound was like a prayer, dying out in the void which spreads between earth and Heaven.

"Let me hold him," she begged.

Because she was the Virgin, even though it might wake him, the Woman did not dare to refuse her. But she asserted her authority, as all mothers must, by pretending that she was the only person who knew how to hold him properly. And perhaps she was the only one at that moment, for there was no other mother besides herself in earth or Heaven. She showed the Virgin how to support his little head because it was wobbly; and how to keep one arm beneath his back because it was weak; and how he liked to be cuddled against her breast because it was warm and cushiony. And then, becoming generous, she taught her the silly little lullaby.

"I shall never go back to Heaven," the Virgin whispered. "I shall stay here always and help you nurse him."

"Never go back to Heaven," the angels echoed; "stay here always."

The Woman's eyes became troubled. "But I want him to myself," she faltered. "I don't want helping." Then she ceased to frown, for she had discovered a stronger argument. "Besides, what about God? You wouldn't leave Him all by Himself in Heaven. He'd be lonely."

The Virgin nodded her head vigorously. "I would, for I also am a woman. There are no babies in Heaven. I couldn't be happy without a baby."

Behind her the angels nodded their haloes. "No babies in Heaven. Couldn't be happy without a baby."

It must have been so much talking that disturbed him; the baby woke up. As he opened his eyes and saw the Queen of Heaven bending over him, he smiled. It was his first smile. On the instant the Woman, like all mothers, became jealous and snatched him back into her own possession. She liked to believe that no one, not even the Man, could make him as comfortable as she could. Piling her golden hair upon her knees to make a pillow for him, she laid him naked on his back and commenced playing with his toes. If he had not given her his first smile, she would at least make certain of his second.

She was so taken up with her playing that she did not notice who had entered. She was the only one who had not noticed. The angels were cowering against the walls of the cave. The Man had roused and crouched covering his face with his hands. Only the Virgin stood upright, meek and fearless, with a look of unconquerable challenge. The Woman was quite oblivious; she went on with her mother-nonsense. And there stood God regarding her through a cloud of puzzlement and anger.

The game that she played with the baby-feet she was inventing on the spur of the moment. Starting with the tiniest toe, she wiggled it. Then she wiggled the next tiniest, and the next tiniest, and the next tiniest, till she had come to the biggest of the tiny toes. To each toe as she wiggled it, she gave a name; when she had wiggled them all she buried her face in the fat, kicking legs.

"And this is Peedy Peedy," she said as she wiggled the littlest toe. "And this next babiest is Polly Loody. And this in the middle is Lady Fissle. And this tall fellow is Lally Vassal.

And last we come of the big, big toe, who's king of them all. His name is Great Ormondon." Then she dived her lips into the little squirming legs and kissed them as if she were going to make a meal of them.

She had to do it four times before the baby smiled at her. At first he only looked serious and astonished.

The fifth time his smile broadened and he gurgled. But the sixth, as she came to "The Great Ormondon," he burst into a crowing laugh. Never before had a laugh been heard in earth or Heaven. It was so surprising that the angels ceased from cowering and the Man uncovered his face to see better.

Then God spoke. His voice was kind and tender like the cooing of doves — so kind and tender that the Woman, discovering His presence, wasn't a bit frightened. Sweeping the hair back from her eyes, she nodded to Him in the old friendly fashion in which she had been used to greet Him in Eden.

"Can you make him do it again?" God asked.

He came nearer and leant above her shoulder. So she made the baby laugh again.

"Could I make him?"

"Try," said the Woman.

So God wiggled the little toes, starting with the tiniest, and the Woman whispered the five magic names to Him secretly so that He might say them all correctly. "Peedy Peedy. Polly Loody. Lady Fissle. Lally Vassal. And the Great Ormondon."

When God boomed out the last large sounding name, the baby doubled his little fists, crowing and laughing unmistakably. Then God laughed, too, and the Virgin, and all the Hosts of Heaven, and the Man and the Woman, till at last the dog and the robin couldn't restrain themselves any longer and joined in His laughter. When once they'd started laughing it was difficult to stop. Besides, they didn't want to stop. They were doing it for the first time and they liked the feeling of it.

God laughed till the tears streamed down His face. By the time He held up His hand for silence, there was scarcely an angel who wasn't wearing his halo crooked.

"That's done us all good," said God. "I must have a baby for my very own exactly like him. I almost think that everybody ought to have babies." Then catching sight of the dog and the robin, He added, "I mean the animals, too."

He turned to the Man. "What day is this? I've not been counting since I ceased to walk in Eden."

The Man answered humbly. "Dear God, it is the twenty-fifth of December."

"I must remember that," said God thoughtfully. And then to the Virgin, "Come. It grows late. There is no one to light the lamps of Heaven. You shall have your desire; for you, too, are a woman."

And the robins say that God did remember, for it was on the twenty-fifth of December, centuries later, that his own son was born into the world. They say that the limestone ridge within sight of Eden was the spot where Bethlehem grew up after Eden vanished.

They even say that the cave to which Mary came on another winter's night, when the doors of the inn had been closed against her, was the very same.

There, where the world's first baby had been born, she wrapped God's son in swaddling clothes and laid him in a manger, for the cave had now become a stable. Perhaps the heavenly host who sang "Peace and Goodwill" to the shepherds was the same, though the robins do not assert that.

Of one thing they are certain: that every time a baby is born God laughs again and His laughter travels down the ages. And that is why on

Christmas Day everyone is especially kind to children, because it was a little child who gave the first laugh and taught grown people, even God Himself, how easy it is to love when one is merry.

THE END

The Glory Of
The Trenches

By

Coningsby Dawson

The Glory Of The Trenches

IN HOSPITAL

Hushed and happy whiteness,
  Miles on miles of cots,
The glad contented brightness
  Where sunlight falls in spots.
Sisters swift and saintly
  Seem to tread on grass;
Like flowers stirring faintly,
  Heads turn to watch them pass.
Beauty, blood, and sorrow,
  Blending in a trance—
Eternity's to-morrow
  In this half-way house of France.
Sounds of whispered talking,
  Laboured indrawn breath;
Then like a young girl walking
  The dear familiar Death

I. THE ROAD TO BLIGHTY

I am in hospital in London, lying between clean white sheets and feeling, for the first time in months, clean all over. At the end of the ward there is a swinging door; if I listen intently in the intervals when the gramophone isn't playing, I can hear the sound of bath-water running—running in a reckless kind of fashion as if it didn't care how much was wasted. To me, so recently out of the fighting and so short a time in Blighty, it seems the finest music in the world. For the sheer luxury of the contrast I close my eyes against the July sunlight and imagine myself back in one of those narrow dug-outs where it isn't the thing to undress because the row may start at any minute.

Out there in France we used to tell one another fairy-tales of how we would spend the first year of life when war was ended. One man had a baby whom he'd never seen; another a girl whom he was anxious to marry. My dream was more prosaic, but no less ecstatic—it began and ended with a large white bed and a large white bath. For the first three hundred and sixty-five mornings after peace had been declared I was to be wakened by the sound of my bath being filled; water was to be so plentiful that I could tumble off to sleep again without even troubling to turn off the tap. In France one has to go dirty so often that the dream of being always clean seems as unrealisable as romance. Our drinking-water is frequently brought up to us at the risk of men's lives, carried through the mud in petrol-cans strapped on to packhorses. To use it carelessly would be like washing in men's blood — —

And here, most marvellously, with my dream come true, I lie in the whitest of white beds. The sunlight filters through trees outside the window and weaves patterns on the floor. Most wonderful of all is the sound of the water so luxuriously running. Some one hops out of bed and re-starts the gramophone. The music of the bath-room tap is lost.

Up and down the ward, with swift precision, nurses move softly. They have the unanxious eyes of those whose days are mapped out with duties. They rarely notice us as individuals. They ask no questions, show no curiosity. Their deeds of persistent kindness are all performed impersonally. It's the same with the doctors. This is a military hospital where discipline is firmly enforced; any natural recognition of common fineness is discouraged. These women who have pledged themselves to live among suffering, never allow themselves for a moment to guess what the sight of them means to us chaps in the cots. Perhaps that also is a part of their sacrifice. But we follow them with our eyes, and we wish that they would allow themselves to guess. For so many months we have not seen a woman; there have been so many hours when we expected never again to see a woman. We're Lazaruses exhumed and restored to normal ways of life by the fluke of having collected a bit of shrapnel — we haven't yet got used to normal ways. The mere rustle of a woman's skirt fills us with unreasonable delight and makes the eyes smart with memories of old longings. Those childish longings of the trenches! No one can understand them who has not been there, where all personal aims are a wash-out and the courage to endure remains one's sole possession.

The sisters at the Casualty Clearing Station — they understood. The Casualty Clearing Station is the first hospital behind the line to which the wounded are brought down straight from the Dressing-Stations. All day and all night ambulances come lurching along shell-torn roads to their doors. The men on the stretchers are still in their bloody tunics, rain-soaked, pain-silent, splashed with the corruption of fighting — their bodies so obviously smashed and their spirits so obviously unbroken. The nurses at the Casualty Clearing Station can scarcely help but understand. They can afford to be feminine to men who are so weak. Moreover, they are near enough the Front to share in the sublime exaltation of those who march out to die. They know when a big offensive is expected, and prepare for it. They are warned the moment it has commenced by the distant thunder of the guns. Then comes the ceaseless stream of lorries and ambulances bringing that which has been broken so quickly to them to be patched up in months. They work day and night with a forgetfulness of self which equals the devotion of the soldiers they are tending. Despite their orderliness they seem almost fanatical in their desire to spend themselves. They are always doing, but they can never do enough. It's the same with the surgeons. I know of one who during a great attack operated for forty-eight hours on end and finally went to sleep where he stood from utter weariness. The picture that forms in my mind of these women is absurd, Arthurian and exact; I see them as great ladies, mediaeval in their saintliness, sharing the pollution of the battle with their champions.

Lying here with nothing to worry about in the green serenity of an English summer, I realize that no man can grasp the splendour of this war until he has made the trip to Blighty on a stretcher. What I mean is this: so long as a fighting man keeps well, his experience of the war consists of muddy roads leading up through a desolated country to holes in the ground, in which he spends most of his time watching other holes in the ground, which people tell him are the Hun front-line. This experience is punctuated by periods during which the earth shoots up about him like corn popping in a pan, and he experiences the insanest fear, if he's made that way, or the most satisfying kind of joy. About once a year something happens which, when it's over, he scarcely believes has happened: he's told that he can run away to England and pretend that there isn't any war on for ten days. For those ten days, so far as he's concerned, hostilities are suspended. He rides post-haste through ravaged villages to the point from which the train starts. Up to the very last moment until the engine pulls out, he's quite panicky lest some one shall come and snatch his warrant from him, telling him that leave has been cancelled. He makes his journey in a carriage in which all the windows are smashed. Probably it either snows or rains. During the night while he stamps his feet to keep warm, he remembers that in his hurry to escape he's left all his Hun souvenirs behind. During his time in London he visits his tailor at least twice a day, buys a vast amount of unnecessary kit, sleeps late, does most of his resting in taxi-cabs, eats innumerable meals at restaurants, laughs at a great many plays in which life at the Front is depicted as a joke. He feels dazed and half suspects that he isn't in London at all, but only dreaming in his dug-out. Some days later he does actually wake up in his dug-out; the only proof he has that he's been on leave is that he can't pay his mess-bill and is minus a hundred pounds. Until a man is wounded he only sees the war from the point of view of the front-line and consequently, as I say, misses half its splendour, for he is ignorant of the greatness of the heart that beats behind him all along the lines of communication. Here in brief is how I found this out.

The dressing-station to which I went was underneath a ruined house, under full observation of the Hun and in an area which was heavily shelled. On account of the shelling and the fact that any movement about the place would attract attention, the wounded were only carried out by night. Moreover, to get back from the dressing-station to the collecting point in rear of the lines, the ambulances had to traverse a white road over a ridge full in view of the enemy. The Huns kept guns trained on this road and opened fire at the least sign of traffic. When I presented myself I didn't think that there was anything seriously the matter; my arm had swelled and was painful from a wound of three days' standing. The doctor, however, recognised that septic poisoning had set in and that to save the arm an operation was necessary without loss of time. He called a sergeant and sent him out to consult with an ambulance-driver. "This officer ought to go out at once. Are you willing to take a chance?" asked the sergeant. The ambulance-driver took a look at the chalk road gleaming white in the sun where it climbed the ridge. "Sure, Mike," he said, and ran off to crank his engine and back his car out of its place of concealment. "Sure, Mike," — that was all. He'd have said the same if he'd been asked whether he'd care to take a chance at Hell.

I have three vivid memories of that drive. The first, my own uneasy sense that I was deserting. Frankly I didn't want to go out; few men do when it comes to the point. The Front has its own peculiar exhilaration, like big game-hunting, discovering the North Pole, or anything that's dangerous; and it has its own peculiar reward — the peace of mind that comes of doing something beyond dispute unselfish and superlatively worth while. It's odd, but it's true that in the front-line many a man experiences peace of mind for the first time and grows a little afraid of a return to normal ways of life. My second memory is of the wistful faces of the chaps whom we passed along the road. At the unaccustomed sound of a car travelling in broad daylight the Tommies poked their heads out of hiding-places like rabbits. Such dirty Tommies! How could they be otherwise living forever on old battlefields? If they were given time for reflection they wouldn't want to go out; they'd choose to stay with the game till the war was ended. But we caught them unaware, and as they gazed after us down the first part of the long trail that leads back from the trenches to Blighty, there was hunger in their eyes. My third memory is of kindness.

You wouldn't think that men would go to war to learn how to be kind — but they do. There's no kinder creature in the whole wide world than the average Tommy. He makes a friend of any stray animal he can find. He shares his last franc with a chap who isn't his pal. He risks his life quite inconsequently to rescue any one who's wounded. When he's gone over the top with bomb and bayonet for the express purpose of "doing in" the Hun, he makes a comrade of the Fritzie he captures. You'll see him coming down the battered trenches with some scared lad of a German at his side. He's gabbling away making throat-noises and signs, smiling and doing his inarticulate best to be intelligible. He pats the Hun on the back, hands him chocolate and cigarettes, exchanges souvenirs and shares with him his last luxury. If any one interferes with his Fritzie he's willing to fight. When they come to the cage where the prisoner has to be handed over, the farewells of these companions whose acquaintance has been made at the bayonet-point are often as absurd as they are affecting. I suppose one only learns the value of kindness when he feels the need of it himself. The men out there have said "Good-bye" to everything they loved, but they've got to love some one—so they give their affections to captured Fritzies, stray dogs, fellows who've collected a piece of a shell—in fact to any one who's a little worse off than themselves. My ambulance-driver was like that with his "Sure, Mike." He was like it during the entire drive. When he came to the white road which climbs the ridge with all the enemy country staring at it, it would have been excusable in him to have hurried. The Hun barrage might descend at any minute. All the way, in the ditches on either side, dead pack animals lay; in the dug-outs there were other unseen dead making the air foul. But he drove slowly and gently, skirting the shell-holes with diligent care so as to spare us every unnecessary jolting. I don't know his name, shouldn't recognise his face, but I shall always remember the almost womanly tenderness of his driving.

After two changes into other ambulances at different distributing points, I arrived about nine on a summer's evening at the Casualty Clearing Station. In something less than an hour I was undressed and on the operating table.

You might suppose that when for three interminable years such a stream of tragedy has flowed through a hospital, it would be easy for surgeons and nurses to treat mutilation and death perfunctorily. They don't. They show no emotion. They are even cheerful; but their strained faces tell the story and their hands have an immense compassion.

Two faces especially loom out. I can always see them by lamp-light, when the rest of the ward is hushed and shrouded, stooping over some silent bed. One face is that of the Colonel of the hospital, grey, concerned, pitiful, stern. His eyes seem to have photographed all the suffering which in three years they have witnessed. He's a tall man, but he moves softly. Over his uniform he wears a long white operating smock—he never seems to remove it. And he never seems to sleep, for he comes wandering through his Gethsemane all hours of the night to bend over the more serious cases. He seems haunted by a vision of the wives, mothers, sweethearts, whose happiness is in his hands. I think of him as a Christ in khaki.

The other face is of a girl—a sister I ought to call her. She's the nearest approach to a sculptured Greek goddess I've seen in a living woman. She's very tall, very pale and golden, with wide brows and big grey eyes like Trilby. I wonder what she did before she went to war—for she's gone to war just as truly as any soldier. I'm sure in the peaceful years she must have spent a lot of time in being loved. Perhaps her man was killed out here. Now she's ivory-white with over-service and spends all her days in loving. Her eyes have the old frank, innocent look, but they're ringed with being weary. Only her lips hold a touch of colour; they have a childish trick of trembling when any one's wound is hurting too much. She's the first touch of home that the stretcher-cases see when they've said good-bye to the trenches. She moves down the ward; eyes follow her. When she is absent, though others take her place, she leaves a loneliness. If she meant much to men in days gone by, to-day she means more than ever. Over many dying boys she stoops as the incarnation of the woman whom, had they lived, they would have loved. To all of us, with the blasphemy of destroying still upon us, she stands for the divinity of womanhood.

What sights she sees and what words she hears; yet the pity she brings to her work preserves her sweetness. In the silence of the night those who are delirious re-fight their recent battles. You're half-asleep, when in the darkened ward some one jumps up in bed, shouting, "Hold your bloody hands up." He thinks he's capturing a Hun trench, taking prisoners in a bombed in dug-out. In an instant, like a mother with a frightened child, she's bending over him; soon she has coaxed his head back on the pillow. Men do not die in vain when they evoke such women. And the men—the chaps in the cots! As a patient the first sight you have of them is a muddy stretcher. The care with which the bearers advance is only equalled by the waiters in old-established London Clubs when they bring in one of their choicest wines. The thing on the stretcher looks horribly like some of the forever silent people you have seen in No Man's Land. A pair of boots you see, a British Warm flung across the body and an arm dragging. A screen is put round a bed; the next sight you have of him is a weary face lying on a white pillow. Soon the chap in the bed next to him is questioning.

"What's yours?"

"Machine-gun caught me in both legs."

"Going to lose 'em?"

"Don't know. Can't feel much at present. Hope not."

Then the questioner raises himself on his elbow. "How's it going?"

It is the attack. The conversation that follows is always how we're hanging on to such and such an objective and have pushed forward three hundred yards here or have been bent back there. One thing you notice: every man forgets his own catastrophe in his keenness for the success of the offensive. Never in all my fortnight's journey to Blighty did I hear a word of self-pity or complaining. On the contrary, the most severely wounded men would profess themselves grateful that they had got off so lightly. Since the war started the term "lightly" has become exceedingly comparative. I suppose a man is justified in saying he's got off lightly when what he expected was death.

I remember a big Highland officer who had been shot in the knee-cap. He had been operated on and the knee-cap had been found to be so splintered that it had had to be removed; of this he was unaware. For the first day as he lay in bed he kept wondering aloud how long it would be before he could re-join his battalion. Perhaps he suspected his condition and was trying to find out. All his heart seemed set on once again getting into the fighting. Next morning he plucked up courage to ask the doctor, and received the answer he had dreaded.

"Never. You won't be going back, old chap."

Next time he spoke his voice was a bit throaty. "Will it stiffen?"

"You've lost the knee-joint," the doctor said, "but with luck we'll save the leg."

His voice sank to a whisper. "If you do, it won't be much good, will it?"

"Not much."

He lay for a couple of hours silent, readjusting his mind to meet the new conditions. Then he commenced talking with cheerfulness about returning to his family. The habit of courage had conquered—the habit of courage which grows out of the knowledge that you let your pals down by showing cowardice.

The next step on the road to Blighty is from the Casualty Station to a Base Hospital in France. You go on a hospital train and are only allowed to go when you are safe to travel. There is always great excitement as to when this event will happen; its precise date usually depends on what's going on up front and the number of fresh casualties which are expected. One morning you awake to find that a tag has been prepared, containing the entire medical history of your injury. The stretcher-bearers come in with grins on their faces, your tag is tied to the top button of your pyjamas, jocular appointments are made by the fellows you leave behind—many of whom you know are dying—to meet you in London, and you are carried out. The train is thoroughly equipped with doctors and nurses; the lying cases travel in little white bunks. No one who has not seen it can have any idea of the high good spirits which prevail. You're going off to Blighty, to Piccadilly, to dry boots and clean beds. The revolving wheels underneath you seem to sing the words, "Off to Blighty—to Blighty." It begins to dawn on you what it will be like to be again your own master and to sleep as long as you like.

Kindness again—always kindness! The sisters on the train can't do enough; they seem to be trying to exceed the self-sacrifice of the sisters you have left behind. You twist yourself so that you can get a glimpse of the flying country. It's green, undisturbed, unmarred by shells — there are even cows!

At the Base Hospital to which I went there was a man who performed miracles. He was a naturalised American citizen, but an Armenian by birth. He gave people new faces.

The first morning an officer came in to visit a friend; his face was entirely swathed in bandages, with gaps left for his breathing and his eyes. He had been like that for two years, and looked like a leper. When he spoke he made hollow noises. His nose and lower jaw had been torn away by an exploding shell. Little by little, with infinite skill, by the grafting of bone and flesh, his face was being built up. Could any surgery be more merciful?

In the days that followed I saw several of these masked men. The worst cases were not allowed to walk about. The ones I saw were invariably dressed with the most scrupulous care in the smartest uniforms, Sam Browns polished and buttons shining. They had hope, and took a pride in themselves — a splendid sign! Perhaps you ask why the face-cases should be kept in France. I was not told, but I can guess — because they dread going back to England to their girls until they've got rid of their disfigurements. So for two years through their bandages they watch the train pull out for Blighty, while the damage which was done them in the fragment of a second is repaired.

At a Base Hospital you see something which you don't see at a Casualty Station — sisters, mothers, sweethearts and wives sitting beside the beds. They're allowed to come over from England when their man is dying. One of the wonderful things to me was to observe how these women in the hour of their tragedy catch the soldier spirit. They're very quiet, very cheerful, very helpful. With passing through the ward they get to know some of the other patients and remember them when they bring their own man flowers. Sometimes when their own man is asleep, they slip over to other bedsides and do something kind for the solitary fellows. That's the army all over; military discipline is based on unselfishness. These women who have been sent for to see their men die, catch from them the spirit of undistressed sacrifice and enrol themselves as soldiers.

Next to my bed there was a Colonel of a north country regiment, a gallant gentleman who positively refused to die. His wife had been with him for two weeks, a little toy woman with nerves worn to a frazzle, who masked her terror with a brave, set smile. The Colonel had had his leg smashed by a whizz-bang when leading his troops into action. Septic poisoning had set in and the leg had been amputated. It had been found necessary to operate several times owing to the poison spreading, with the result that, being far from a young man, his strength was exhausted. Men forgot their own wounds in watching this one man's fight for life. He became symbolic of what, in varying degrees, we were all doing. When he was passing through a crisis the whole ward waited breathless. There was the finest kind of rivalry between the night and day sisters to hand him over at the end of each twelve hours with his pulse stronger and temperature lower than when they received him. Each was sure she had the secret of keeping him alive.

You discovered the spirit of the man when you heard him wandering in delirium. All night in the shadowy ward with its hooded lamps, he would be giving orders for the comfort of his men. Sometimes he'd be proposing to go forward himself to a place where a company was having a hot time; apparently one of his officers was trying to dissuade him. "Danger be damned," he'd exclaim in a wonderfully strong voice. "It'll buck 'em up to see me. Splendid chaps—splendid chaps!"

About dawn he was usually supposed to be sinking, but he'd rallied again by the time the day-sister arrived. "Still here," he'd smile in a triumphant kind of whisper, as though bluffing death was a pastime.

One afternoon a padre came to visit him. As he was leaving he bent above the pillow. We learnt afterwards that this was what he had said, "If the good Lord lets you, I hope you'll get better."

We saw the Colonel raise himself up on his elbow. His weak voice shook with anger. "Neither God nor the Devil has anything to do with it. I'm going to get well." Then, as the nurse came hurrying to him, he sank back.

When I left the Base Hospital for Blighty he was still holding his own. I have never heard what happened to him, but should not be at all surprised to meet him one day in the trenches with a wooden leg, still leading his splendid chaps. Death can't kill men of such heroic courage.

At the Base Hospital they talk a good deal of "the Blighty Smile." It's supposed to be the kind of look a chap wears when he's been told that within twenty-four hours he'll be in England. When this information has been imparted to him, he's served out with warm socks, woollen cap and a little linen bag into which to put his valuables. Hours and hours before there's any chance of starting you'll see the lucky ones lying very still, with a happy vacant look in their eyes and their absurd woollen caps stuck ready on their heads. Sometime, perhaps in the small hours of the morning, the stretcher-bearers, arrive—the stretcher-bearers who all down the lines of communication are forever carrying others towards blessedness and never going themselves. "At last," you whisper to yourself. You feel a glorious anticipation that you have not known since childhood when, after three hundred and sixty-four days of waiting, it was truly going to be Christmas.

On the train and on the passage there is the same skillful attention—the same ungrudging kindness. You see new faces in the bunks beside you. After the tedium of the narrow confines of a ward that in itself is exciting. You fall into talk.

"What's yours?"

"Nothing much—just a hand off and a splinter or two in the shoulder."

You laugh. "That's not so dusty. How much did you expect for your money?"

Probably you meet some one from the part of the line where you were wounded—with luck even from your own brigade, battery or battalion. Then the talk becomes all about how things are going, whether we're still holding on to our objectives, who's got a blighty and who's gone west. One discussion you don't often hear—as to when the war will end. To these civilians in khaki it seems that the war has always been and that they will never cease to be soldiers. For them both past and future are utterly obliterated. They would not have it otherwise. Because they are doing their duty they are contented. The only time the subject is ever touched on is when some one expresses the hope that it'll last long enough for him to recover from his wounds and get back into the line. That usually starts another man, who will never be any more good for the trenches, wondering whether he can get into the flying corps. The one ultimate hope of all these shattered wrecks who are being hurried to the Blighty they have dreamt of, is that they may again see service.

The tang of salt in the air, the beat of waves and then, incredible even when it has been realised, England. I think they ought to make the hospital trains which run to London all of glass, then instead of watching little triangles of flying country by leaning uncomfortably far out of their bunks, the wounded would be able to drink their full of the greenness which they have longed for so many months. The trees aren't charred and blackened stumps; they're harps between the knees of the hills, played on by the wind and sun. The villages have their roofs on and children romping in their streets. The church spires haven't been knocked down; they stand up tall and stately. The roadsides aren't littered with empty shell-cases and dead horses. The fields are absolutely fields, with green crops, all wavy, like hair growing. After the tonsured filth we've been accustomed to call a world, all this strikes one as unnatural and extraordinary. There's a sweet fragrance over everything and one's throat feels lumpy. Perhaps it isn't good for people's health to have lumpy throats, and that's why they don't run glass trains to London.

Then, after such excited waiting, you feel that the engine is slowing down. There's a hollow rumbling; you're crossing the dear old wrinkled Thames. If you looked out you'd see the dome of St. Paul's like a bubble on the sky-line and smoking chimneys sticking up like thumbs — things quite ugly and things of surpassing beauty, all of which you have never hoped to see again and which in dreams you have loved. But if you could look out, you wouldn't have the time. You're getting your things together, so you won't waste a moment when they come to carry you out. Very probably you're secreting a souvenir or two about your person: something you've smuggled down from the front which will really prove to your people that you've made the acquaintance of the Hun. As though your wounds didn't prove that sufficiently. Men are childish.

The engine comes to a halt. You can smell the cab-stands. You're really there. An officer comes through the train enquiring whether you have any preference as to hospitals. Your girl lives in Liverpool or Glasgow or Birmingham. Good heavens, the fellow holds your destiny in his hands! He can send you to Whitechapel if he likes. So, even though he has the same rank as yourself, you address him as, "Sir."

Perhaps it's because I've practised this diplomacy—I don't know. Anyway, he's granted my request. I'm to stay in London. I was particularly anxious to stay in London, because one of my young brothers from the Navy is there on leave at present. In fact he wired me to France that the Admiralty had allowed him a three-days' special extension of leave in order that he might see me. It was on the strength of this message that the doctors at the Base Hospital permitted me to take the journey several days before I was really in a condition to travel.

I'm wondering whether he's gained admission to the platform. I lie there in my bunk all eyes, expecting any minute to see him enter. Time and again I mistake the blue serge uniform of the St. John's Ambulance for that of a naval lieutenant. They come to carry me out. What an extraordinarily funny way to enter London—on a stretcher! I've arrived on boat-trains from America, troop trains from Canada, and come back from romantic romps in Italy, but never in my wildest imaginings did I picture myself arriving as a wounded soldier on a Red Cross train.

Still clutching my absurd linen bag, which contains my valuables, I lift my head from the pillow gazing round for any glimpse of that much-desired brother. Now they've popped me onto the upper-shelf of a waiting ambulance; I can see nothing except what lies out at the back. I at once start explaining to the nurse who accompanies us that I've lost a very valuable brother—that he's probably looking for me somewhere on the station. She's extremely sympathetic and asks the chauffeur to drive very slowly so that we may watch for him as we go through the station gates into the Strand.

We're delayed for some minutes while particulars are checked up of our injuries and destinations. The lying cases are placed four in an ambulance, with the flap raised at the back so we can see out. The sitting cases travel in automobiles, buses and various kinds of vehicles. In my ambulance there are two leg-cases with most theatrical bandages, and one case of trench-fever. We're immensely merry—all except the trench-fever case who has conceived an immense sorrow for himself. We get impatient with waiting. There's an awful lot of cheering going on somewhere; we suppose troops are marching and can't make it out.

Ah, we've started! At a slow crawl to prevent jarring we pass through the gates. We discover the meaning of the cheering. On either side the people are lined in dense crowds, waving and shouting. It's Saturday evening when they should be in the country. It's jolly decent of them to come here to give us such a welcome. Flower-girls are here with their baskets full of flowers—just poor girls with a living to earn. They run after us as we pass and strew us with roses. Roses! We stretch out our hands, pressing them to our lips. How long is it since we held roses in our hands? How did these girls of the London streets know that above all things we longed for flowers? It was worth it all, the mud and stench and beastliness, when it was to this that the road led back. And the girls—they're even better than the flowers; so many pretty faces made kind by compassion. Somewhere inside ourselves we're laughing; we're so happy. We don't need any one's pity; time enough for that when we start to pity ourselves. We feel mean, as though we were part of a big deception. We aren't half so ill as we look; if you put sufficient bandages on a wound you can make the healthiest man appear tragic. We're laughing—and then all of a sudden we're crying. We press our faces against the pillow ashamed of ourselves. We won't see the crowds; we're angry with them for having unmanned us. And then we can't help looking; their love reaches us almost as though it were the touch of hands. We won't hide ourselves if we mean so much to them. We're not angry any more, but grateful.

Suddenly the ambulance-nurse shouts to the driver. The ambulance stops. She's quite excited. Clutching me with one hand, she points with the other, "There he is."

"Who?"

I raise myself. A naval lieutenant is standing against the pavement, gazing anxiously at the passing traffic.

"Your brother, isn't it?"

I shook my head. "Not half handsome enough."

For the rest of the journey she's convinced I have a headache. It's no good telling her that I haven't; much to my annoyance and amusement she swabs my forehead with eau-de-Cologne, telling me that I shall soon feel better.

The streets through which we pass are on the south side of the Thames. It's Saturday evening. Hawkers' barrows line the kerb; women with draggled skirts and once gay hats are doing their Sunday shopping. We're having a kind of triumphant procession; with these people to feel is to express. We catch some of their remarks: "'Oo! Look at 'is poor leg!" "My, but ain't 'e done in shockin'!"

Dear old London—so kind, so brave, so frankly human! You're just like the chaps at the Front—you laugh when you suffer and give when you're starving; you never know when not to be generous. You wear your heart in your eyes and your lips are always ready for kissing, I think of you as one of your own flower-girls—hoarse of voice, slatternly as to corsets, with a big tumbled fringe over your forehead, and a heart so big that you can chuck away your roses to a wounded Tommy and go away yourself with an empty basket to sleep under an archway. Do you wonder that to us you spell Blighty? We love you.

We come to a neighbourhood more respectable and less demonstrative, skirt a common, are stopped at a porter's lodge and turn into a parkland. The glow of sunset is ended; the blue-grey of twilight is settling down. Between flowered borders we pick our way, pause here and there for directions and at last halt. Again the stretcher-bearers! As I am carried in I catch a glimpse of a low bungalow-building, with others like it dotted about beneath trees. There are red shaded lamps. Every one tiptoes in silence. Only the lips move when people speak; there is scarcely any sound. As the stretchers are borne down the ward men shift their heads to gaze after them. It's past ten o'clock and patients are supposed to be sleeping now. I'm put to bed. There's no news of my brother; he hasn't 'phoned and hasn't called. I persuade one of the orderlies to ring up the hotel at which I know he was staying. The man is a long while gone. Through the dim length of the ward I watch the door into the garden, momentarily expecting the familiar figure in the blue uniform and gold buttons to enter. He doesn't. Then at length the orderly returns to tell me that the naval lieutenant who was staying at the hotel, had to set out for his ship that evening, as there was no train that he could catch on Sunday. So he was steaming out of London for the North at the moment I was entering. Disappointed? Yes. One shrugs his shoulders. C'est la guerre, as we say in the trenches. You can't have everything when Europe's at war.

I can hardly keep awake long enough for the sister to dress my arm. The roses that the flower-girls had thrown me are in water and within handstretch. They seem almost persons and curiously sacred—symbols of all the heroism and kindness that has ministered to me every step of the journey. It's a good little war I think to myself. Then, with the green smell of England in my nostrils and the rumbling of London in my ears, like conversation below stairs, I drowse off into the utter contentment of the first deep sleep I have had since I was wounded.

I am roused all too soon by some one sticking a thermometer into my mouth. Rubbing my eyes, I consult my watch. Half-past five! Rather early! Raising myself stealthily, I catch a glimpse of a neat little sister darting down the ward from bed to bed, tent-pegging every sleeping face with a fresh thermometer. Having made the round, back she comes to take possession of my hand while she counts my pulse. I try to speak, but she won't let me remove the accursed thermometer; when she has removed it herself, off she goes to the next bed. I notice that she has auburn hair, merry blue eyes and a ripping Irish accent. I learn later that she's a Sinn

Feiner, a sworn enemy to England who sings "Dark Rosaleen" and other rebel songs in the secret watches of the night. It seems to me that in taking care of England's wounded she's solving the Irish problem pretty well.

Heavens, she's back again, this time with a bowl of water and a towel! Very severely and thoroughly, as though I were a dirty urchin, she scrubs my face and hands. She even brushes my hair. I watch her do the same for other patients, some of whom are Colonels and old enough to be her father. She's evidently in no mood for proposals of marriage at this early hour, for her technique is impartially severe to everybody, though her blue eyes are unfailingly laughing.

It is at this point that somebody crawls out of bed, slips into a dressing-gown, passes through the swing door at the end of the ward and sets the bath-water running. The sound of it is ecstatic.

Very soon others follow his example. They're chaps without legs, with an arm gone, a hand gone, back wounds, stomach wounds, holes in the head. They start chaffing one another. There's no hint of tragedy. A gale of laughter sweeps the ward from end to end. An Anzac captain is called on for a speech. I discover that he is our professional comic man and is called on to make speeches twenty times a day. They always start with, "Gentlemen, I will say this—" and end with a flourish in praise of Australia. Soon the ward is made perilous by wheel-chairs, in which unskilful pilots steer themselves out into the green adventure of the garden. Birds are singing out there; the guns had done for the birds in the places where we came from. Through open doors we can see the glow of flowers, dew-laden and sparkling, lazily unfolding their petals in the early sun.

When the sister's back is turned, a one-legged officer nips out of bed and hops like a crow to the gramophone. The song that follows is a favourite. Curious that it should be, for it paints a dream which to many of these mutilated men—Canadians, Australians, South Africans, Imperials—will have to remain only a dream, so long as life lasts. Girls don't marry fellows without arms and legs—at least they didn't in peace days before the world became heroic. As the gramophone commences to sing, heads on pillows hum the air and fingers tap in time on the sheets. It's a peculiarly childish song for men who have seen what they have seen and done what they have done, to be so fond of. Here's the way it runs:—

"We'll have a little cottage in a little town

 And well have a little mistress in a dainty gown,

 A little doggie, a little cat,

 A little doorstep with WELCOME on the mat;

 And we'll have a little trouble and a little strife,

 But none of these things matter when you've got a little wife.

 We shall be as happy as the angels up above

 With a little patience and a lot of love."

A little patience and a lot of love! I suppose that's the line that's caught the chaps. Behind all their smiling and their boyish gaiety they know that they'll need both patience and love to meet the balance of existence with sweetness and soldierly courage. It won't be so easy to be soldiers when they get back into mufti and go out into the world cripples. Here in their pyjamas in the summer sun, they're making a first class effort. I take another look at them. No, there'll never be any whining from men such as these.

Some of us will soon be back in the fighting—and jolly glad of it. Others are doomed to remain in the trenches for the rest of their lives—not the trenches of the front-line where they've been strafed by the Hun, but the trenches of physical curtailment where self-pity will launch wave after wave of attack against them. It won't be easy not to get the "wind up." It'll be difficult to maintain normal cheerfulness. But they're not the men they were before they went to war—out there they've learnt something. They're game. They'll remain soldiers, whatever happens.

THE LADS AWAY

All the lads have gone out to play

At being soldiers, far away;

They won't be back for many a day,

And some won't be back any morning.

All the lassies who laughing were

When hearts were light and lads were here,

Go sad-eyed, wandering hither and there—

They pray and they watch for the morning.

Every house has its vacant bed

And every night, when sounds are dead,

Some woman yearns for the pillowed head

Of him who marched out in the morning.

Of all the lads who've gone out to play

There's some'll return and some who'll stay;

There's some will be back 'most any day—

But some won't wake up in the morning.

II. THE GROWING OF THE VISION

I'm continuing in America the book which I thought out during the golden July and August days when I lay in the hospital in London. I've been here a fortnight; everything that's happened seems unbelievably wonderful, as though it had happened to some one other than myself. It'll seem still more wonderful in a few weeks' time when I'm where I hope I shall be—back in the mud at the Front.

Here's how this miraculous turn of events occurred. When I went before my medical board I was declared unfit for active service for at least two months. A few days later I went in to General Headquarters to see what were the chances of a trip to New York. The officer whom I consulted pulled out his watch, "It's noon now. There's a boat-train leaving Euston in two and a half hours. Do you think you can pack up and make it?"

Did I think!

"You watch me," I cried.

Dashing out into Regent Street I rounded up a taxi and raced about London like one possessed, collecting kit, visiting tailors, withdrawing money, telephoning friends with whom I had dinner and theatre engagements. It's an extraordinary characteristic of the Army, but however hurried an officer may be, he can always spare time to visit his tailor. The fare I paid my taxi-driver was too monstrous for words; but then he'd missed his lunch, and one has to miss so many things in war-times that when a new straw of inconvenience is piled on the camel, the camel expects to be compensated. Anyway, I was on that boat-train when it pulled out of London.

I was in uniform when I arrived in New York, for I didn't possess any mufti. You can't guess what a difference that made to one's home-coming — not the being in uniform, but the knowing that it wasn't an offence to wear it. On my last leave, some time ago before I went overseas, if I'd tried to cross the border from Canada in uniform I'd have been turned back; if by any chance I'd got across and worn regimentals I'd have been arrested by the first Irish policeman. A place isn't home where you get turned back or locked up for wearing the things of which you're proudest. If America hadn't come into the war none of us who have loved her and since been to the trenches, would ever have wanted to return.

But she's home now as she never was before and never could have been under any other circumstances—now that khaki strides unabashed down Broadway and the skirl of the pipers has been heard on Fifth Avenue. We men "over there" will have to find a new name for America. It won't be exactly Blighty, but a kind of very wealthy first cousin to Blighty—a word meaning something generous and affectionate and steam-heated, waiting for us on the other side of the Atlantic.

Two weeks here already—two weeks more to go; then back to the glory of the trenches!

There's one person I've missed since my return to New York. I've caught glimpses of him disappearing around corners, but he dodges. I think he's a bit ashamed to meet me. That person is my old civilian self. What a full-blown egoist he used to be! How full of golden plans for his own advancement! How terrified of failure, of disease, of money losses, of death—of all the temporary, external, non-essential things that have nothing to do with the spirit! War is in itself damnable—a profligate misuse of the accumulated brain-stuff of centuries. Nevertheless, there's many a man who has no love of war, who previous to the war had cramped his soul with littleness and was chased by the bayonet of duty into the blood-stained largeness of the trenches, who has learnt to say, "Thank God for this war." He thanks God not because of the carnage, but because when the wine-press of new ideals was being trodden, he was born in an age when he could do his share.

America's going through just about the same experience as myself. She's feeling broader in the chest, bigger in the heart and her eyes are clearer. When she catches sight of the America that she was, she's filled with doubt—she can't believe that that person with the Stars and Stripes wrapped round her and a money-bag in either hand ever was herself. Home, clean and honourable for every man who ever loved her and has pledged his life for an ideal with the Allies—that's what she's become now.

I read again the words that I wrote about those chaps in the London hospital, men who had journeyed to their Calvary glad-hearted from the farthest corners of the world. From this distance I see them in truer perspective than when we lay companions side by side in that long line of neat, white cots. I used to grope after ways to explain them—to explain the courage which in their utter heroism they did not realise they possessed. They had grown so accustomed to a brave way of living that they sincerely believed they were quite ordinary persons. That's courage at its finest— when it becomes unconscious and instinctive.

At first I said, "I know why they're so cheerful—it's because they're all here in one ward together. They're all mutilated more or less, so they don't feel that they're exceptional. It's as though the whole world woke up with toothache one morning. At breakfast every one would be feeling very sorry for himself; by lunch-time, when it had become common knowledge that the entire world had the same kind of ache, toothache would have ceased to exist. It's the loneliness of being abnormal in your suffering that hurts."

But it wasn't that. Even while I was confined to the hospital, in hourly contact with the chaps, I felt that it wasn't that. When I was allowed to dress and go down West for a few hours everyday, I knew that I was wrong most certainly. In Piccadilly, Hyde Park, theatres, restaurants, river-places on the Thames you'd see them, these men who were maimed for life, climbing up and down buses, hobbling on their crutches independently through crowds, hailing one another cheerily from taxis, drinking life joyously in big gulps without complaint or sense of martyrdom, and getting none of the dregs. A part of their secret was that through their experience in the trenches they had learnt to be self-forgetful. The only time I ever saw a wounded man lose his temper was when some one out of kindness made him remember himself. A sudden down-pour of rain had commenced; it was towards evening and all the employees of the West End shopping centre were making haste to get home to the suburbs. A young Highland officer who had lost a leg scrambled into a bus going to Wandsworth. The inside of the bus was jammed, so he had to stand up clutching on to a strap. A middle-aged gentleman rose from his seat and offered it to the Highlander. The Highlander smiled his thanks and shook his head. The middle-aged gentleman in his sympathy became pressing, attracting attention to the officer's infirmity. It was then that the officer lost his temper. I saw him flush.

"I don't want it," he said sharply. "There's nothing the matter with me. Thanks all the same. I'll stand."

This habit of being self-forgetful gives one time to be remindful of others. Last January, during a brief and glorious ten days' leave, I went to a matinée at the Coliseum. Vesta Tilley was doing an extraordinarily funny impersonation of a Tommy just home from the comfort of the trenches; her sketch depicted the terrible discomforts of a fighting man on leave in Blighty. If I remember rightly the refrain of her song ran somewhat in this fashion:

"Next time they want to give me six days' leave

 Let 'em make it six months' 'ard."

There were two officers, a major and a captain, behind us; judging by the sounds they made, they were getting their full money's worth of enjoyment. In the interval, when the lights went up, I turned and saw the captain putting a cigarette between the major's lips; then, having gripped a match-box between his knees so that he might strike the match, he lit the cigarette for his friend very awkwardly. I looked closer and discovered that the laughing captain had only one hand and the equally happy major had none at all.

Men forget their own infirmities in their endeavour to help each other. Before the war we had a phrase which has taken on a new meaning now; we used to talk about "lending a hand." To-day we lend not only hands, but arms and eyes and legs. The wonderful comradeship learnt in the trenches has taught men to lend their bodies to each other—out of two maimed bodies to make up one which is whole, and sound, and shared. You saw this all the time in hospital. A man who had only one leg would pal up with a man who had only one arm. The one-armed man would wheel the one-legged man about the garden in a chair; at meal-times the one-legged man would cut up the one-armed man's food for him. They had both lost something, but by pooling what was left they managed to own a complete body. By the time the war is ended there'll be great hosts of helpless men who by combining will have learnt how to become helpful. They'll establish a new standard of very simple and cheerful socialism.

There's a point I want to make clear before I forget it. All these men, whether they're capturing Hun dug-outs at the Front or taking prisoner their own despair in English hospitals, are perfectly ordinary and normal. Before the war they were shop-assistants, cab-drivers, plumbers, lawyers, vaudeville artists. They were men of no heroic training. Their civilian callings and their previous social status were too various for any one to suppose that they were heroes ready-made at birth. Something has happened to them since they marched away in khaki—something that has changed them. They're as completely re-made as St. Paul was after he had had his vision of the opening heavens on the road to Damascus. They've brought their vision back with them to civilian life, despite the lost arms and legs which they scarcely seem to regret; their souls still triumph over the body and the temporal. As they hobble through the streets of London, they display the same gay courage that was theirs when at zero hour, with a fifty-fifty chance of death, they hopped over the top for the attack.

Often at the Front I have thought of Christ's explanation of his own unassailable peace—an explanation given to his disciples at the Last Supper, immediately before the walk to Gethsemane: "Be of good cheer, I have overcome the world." Overcoming the world, as I understand it, is overcoming self. Fear, in its final analysis, is nothing but selfishness. A man who is afraid in an attack, isn't thinking of his pals and how quickly terror spreads; he isn't thinking of the glory which will accrue to his regiment or division if the attack is a success; he isn't thinking of what he can do to contribute to that success; he isn't thinking of the splendour of forcing his spirit to triumph over weariness and nerves and the abominations that the Huns are chucking at him. He's thinking merely of how he can save his worthless skin and conduct his entirely unimportant body to a place where there aren't any shells.

In London as I saw the work-a-day, unconscious nobility of the maimed and wounded, the words, "I have overcome the world," took an added depth. All these men have an "I-have-overcome-the-world" look in their faces. It's comparatively easy for a soldier with traditions and ideals at his back to face death calmly; to be calm in the face of life, as these chaps are, takes a graver courage.

What has happened to change them? These disabilities, had they happened before the war, would have crushed and embittered them. They would have been woes utterly and inconsolably unbearable. Intrinsically their physical disablements spell the same loss to-day that they would have in 1912. The attitude of mind in which they are accepted alone makes them seem less. This attitude of mind or greatness of soul—whatever you like to call it—was learnt in the trenches where everything outward is polluted and damnable. Their experience at the Front has given them what in the Army language is known as "guts." "Guts" or courage is an attitude of mind towards calamity—an attitude of mind which makes the honourable accomplishing of duty more permanently satisfying than the preservation of self. But how did this vision come to these men? How did they rid themselves of their civilian flabbiness and acquire it? These questions are best answered autobiographically. Here briefly, is the story of the growth of the vision within myself.

In August, 1914, three days after war had been declared, I sailed from Quebec for England on the first ship that put out from Canada. The trip had been long planned—it was not undertaken from any patriotic motive. My family, which included my father, mother, sister and brother, had been living in America for eight years and had never returned to England together. It was the accomplishing of a dream long cherished, which favourable circumstances and a sudden influx of money had at last made possible. We had travelled three thousand miles from our ranch in the Rockies before the war-cloud burst; obstinacy and curiosity combined made us go on, plus an entirely British feeling that by crossing the Atlantic during the crisis we'd be showing our contempt for the Germans.

We were only informed that the ship was going to sail at the very last moment, and went aboard in the evening. The word spread quickly among the crews of other vessels lying in harbour; their firemen, keen to get back to England and have a whack at the Huns, tried to board our ship, sometimes by a ruse, more often by fighting. One saw some very pretty fist work that night as he leant across the rail, wondering whether he'd ever reach the other side. There were rumours of German warships waiting to catch us in mid-ocean. Somewhere towards midnight the would-be stowaways gave up their attempt to force a passage; they squatted with their backs against the sheds along the quayside, singing patriotic songs to the accompaniment of mouth-organs, confidently asserting that they were sons of the bull-dog breed and never, never would be slaves. It was all very amusing; war seemed to be the finest of excuses for an outburst of high spirits.

Next morning, when we came on deck for a breath of air the vessel was under way; all hands were hard at work disguising her with paint of a sombre colour. Here and there you saw an officer in uniform, who had not yet had time to unpack his mufti. The next night, and for the rest of the voyage, all port-holes were darkened and we ran without lights. An atmosphere of suspense became omnipresent. Rumours spread like wild-fire of sinkings, victories, defeats, marching and countermarchings, engagements on land and water. With the uncanny and unaccustomed sense of danger we began to realise that we, as individuals, were involved in a European war.

As we got about among the passengers we found that the usual spirit of comradeship which marks an Atlantic voyage, was noticeably lacking. Every person regarded every other person with distrust, as though he might be a spy. People were secretive as to their calling and the purpose of their voyage; little by little we discovered that many of them were government officials, but that most were professional soldiers rushing back in the hope that they might be in time to join the British Expeditionary Force. Long before we had guessed that a world tragedy was impending, they had judged war's advent certain from its shadow, and had come from the most distant parts of Canada that they might be ready to embark the moment the cloud burst. Some of them were travelling with their wives and children. What struck me as wholly unreasonable was that these professional soldiers and their families were the least disturbed people on board. I used to watch them as one might watch condemned prisoners in their cells. Their apparent indifference was unintelligible to me. They lived their daily present, contented and unruffled, just as if it were going to be their present always. I accused them of being lacking in imagination. I saw them lying dead on battlefields. I saw them dragging on into old age, with the spine of life broken, mutilated and mauled. I saw them in desperately tight corners, fighting in ruined villages with sword and bayonet. But they joked, laughed, played with their kiddies and seemed to have no realisation of the horrors to which they were going. There was a world-famous aviator, who had gone back on his marriage promise that he would abandon his aerial adventures. He was hurrying to join the French Flying Corps. He and his young wife used to play deck-tennis every morning as lightheartedly as if they were travelling to Europe for a lark. In my many accusations of these men's indifference I never accused them of courage.

Courage, as I had thought of it up to that time, was a grim affair of teeth set, sad eyes and clenched hands—the kind of "My head is bloody but unbowed" determination described in Henley's poem.

When we had arrived safe in port we were held up for some time. A tug came out, bringing a lot of artificers who at once set to work tearing out the fittings of the ship that she might be converted into a transport. Here again I witnessed a contrast between the soldierly and the civilian attitude. The civilians, with their easily postponed engagements, fumed and fretted at the delay in getting ashore. The officers took the inconvenience with philosophical good-humour. While the panelling and electric-light fittings were being ripped out, they sat among the debris and played cards. There was heaps of time for their appointment—it was only with wounds and Death. To me, as a civilian, their coolness was almost irritating and totally incomprehensible. I found a new explanation by saying that, after all, war was their professional chance—in fact, exactly what a shortage in the flour-market was to a man who had quantities of wheat on hand.

That night we travelled to London, arriving about two o'clock in the morning. There was little to denote that a European war was on, except that people were a trifle more animated and cheerful. The next day was Sunday, and we motored round Hampstead Heath. The Heath was as usual, gay with pleasure-seekers and the streets sedate with church-goers. On Monday, when we tried to transact business and exchange money, we found that there were hitches and difficulties; it was more as though a window had been left open and a certain untidiness had resulted. "It will be all right tomorrow," everybody said. "Business as usual," and they nodded.

But as the days passed it wasn't all right. Kitchener began to call for his army. Belgium was invaded. We began to hear about atrocities. There were rumours of defeat, which ceased to be rumours, and of grey hordes pressing towards Paris. It began to dawn on the most optimistic of us that the little British Army—the Old Contemptibles—hadn't gone to France on a holiday jaunt.

The sternness of the hour was brought home to me by one obscure incident. Straggling across Trafalgar Square in mufti and commanded by a sergeant came a little procession of recruits. They were roughly dressed men of the navy and the coster class. All save one carried under his arm his worldly possessions, wrapped in cloth, brown-paper or anything that had come handy. The sergeant kept on giving them the step and angrily imploring them to pick it up. At the tail of the procession followed a woman; she also carried a package.

They turned into the Strand, passed by Charing Cross and branched off to the right down a lane to the Embankment. At the point where they left the Strand, the man without a parcel spoke to the sergeant and fell out of the ranks. He laid his clumsy hand on the woman's arm; she set down on the pavement the parcel she had been carrying. There they stood for a full minute gazing at each other dumbly, oblivious to the passing crowds. She wasn't pleasing to look at—just a slum woman with draggled skirts, a shawl gathered tightly round her and a mildewed kind of bonnet. He was no more attractive—a hulking Samson, perhaps a day-labourer, who whilst he had loved her, had probably beaten her. They had come to the hour of parting, and there they stood in the London sunshine inarticulate after life together. He glanced after the procession; it was two hundred yards away by now. Stooping awkwardly for the burden which she had carried for him, in a shame-faced kind of way he kissed her; then broke from her to follow his companions. She watched him forlornly, her hands hanging empty. Never once did he look back as he departed. Catching up, he took his place in the ranks; they rounded a corner and were lost. Her eyes were quite dry; her jaw sagged stupidly. For some seconds she stared after the way he had gone—her man! Then she wandered off as one who had no purpose.

Wounded men commenced to appear in the streets. You saw them in restaurants, looking happy and embarrassed, being paraded by proud families. One day I met two in my tailor's shop—one had an arm in a sling, the other's head had been seared by a bullet. It was whispered that they were officers who had "got it" at Mons. A thrill ran through me—a thrill of hero-worship.

At the Empire Music Hall in Leicester Square, tragedy bared its broken teeth and mouthed at me. We had reached the stage at which we had become intensely patriotic by the singing of songs. A beautiful actress, who had no thought of doing "her bit" herself, attired as Britannia, with a colossal Union Jack for background, came before the footlights and sang the recruiting song of the moment,

"We don't want to lose you

 But we think you ought to go."

Some one else recited a poem calculated to shame men into immediate enlistment, two lines of which I remember:

"I wasn't among the first to go

 But I went, thank God, I went."

The effect of such urging was to make me angry. I wasn't going to be rushed into khaki on the spur of an emotion picked up in a music-hall. I pictured the comfortable gentlemen, beyond the military age, who had written these heroic taunts, had gained reputation by so doing, and all the time sat at home in suburban security. The people who recited or sung their effusions, made me equally angry; they were making sham-patriotism a means of livelihood and had no intention of doing their part. All the world that by reason of age or sex was exempt from the ordeal of battle, was shoving behind all the rest of the world that was not exempt, using the younger men as a shield against his own terror and at the same time calling them cowards. That was how I felt. I told myself that if I went—and the if seemed very remote—I should go on a conviction and not because of shoving. They could hand me as many white feathers as they liked, I wasn't going to be swept away by the general hysteria. Besides, where would be the sense in joining? Everybody said that our fellows would be home for Christmas. Our chaps who were out there ought to know; in writing home they promised it themselves.

The next part of the music-hall performance was moving pictures of the Germans' march into Brussels. I was in the Promenade and had noticed a Belgian soldier being made much of by a group of Tommies. He was a queer looking fellow, with a dazed expression and eyes that seemed to focus on some distant horror; his uniform was faded and torn—evidently it had seen active service. I wondered by what strange fortune he had been conveyed from the brutalities of invasion to this gilded, plush-seated sensation-palace in Leicester Square.

I watched the screen. Through ghastly photographic boulevards the spectre conquerors marched. They came on endlessly, as though somewhere out of sight a human dam had burst, whose deluge would never be stopped. I tried to catch the expressions of the men, wondering whether this or that or the next had contributed his toll of violated women and butchered children to the list of Hun atrocities. Suddenly the silence of the theatre was startled by a low, infuriated growl, followed by a shriek which was hardly human. I have since heard the same kind of sounds when the stumps of the mutilated are being dressed and the pain has become intolerable. Everybody turned in their seats—gazing through the dimness to a point in the Promenade near to where I was. The ghosts on the screen were forgotten. The faked patriotism of the songs we had listened to had become a thing of naught. Through the welter of bombast, excitement and emotion we had grounded on reality.

The Belgian soldier, in his tattered uniform, was leaning out, as though to bridge the space that divided him from his ghostly tormentors. The dazed look was gone from his expression and his eyes were focussed in the fixity of a cruel purpose—to kill, and kill, and kill the smoke-grey hordes of tyrants so long as his life should last. He shrieked imprecations at them, calling upon God and snatching epithets from the gutter in his furious endeavour to curse them. He was dragged away by friends in khaki, overpowered, struggling, smothered but still cursing.

I learnt afterwards that he, with his mother and two brothers, had been the proprietors of one of the best hotels in Brussels. Both his brothers had been called to arms and were dead. Anything might have happened to his mother—he had not heard from her. He himself had escaped in the general retreat and was going back to France as interpreter with an English regiment. He had lost everything; it was the sight of his ruined hotel, flung by chance on the screen, that had provoked his demonstration. He was dead to every emotion except revenge—to accomplish which he was returning.

The moving-pictures still went on; nobody had the heart to see more of them. The house rose, fumbling for its coats and hats; the place was soon empty.

Just as I was leaving a recruiting sergeant touched my elbow, "Going to enlist, sonny?"

I shook my head. "Not to-night. Want to think it over."

"You will," he said. "Don't wait too long. We can make a man of you. If I get you in my squad I'll give you hell."

I didn't doubt it.

I don't know that I'm telling these events in their proper sequence as they led up to the growing of the vision. That doesn't matter—the point is that the conviction was daily strengthening that I was needed out there. The thought was grotesque that I could ever make a soldier—I whose life from the day of leaving college had been almost wholly sedentary. In fights at school I could never hurt the other boy until by pain he had stung me into madness. Moreover, my idea of war was grimly graphic; I thought it consisted of a choice between inserting a bayonet into some one else's stomach or being yourself the recipient. I had no conception of the long-distance, anonymous killing that marks our modern methods, and is in many respects more truly awful. It's a fact that there are hosts of combatants who have never once identified the bodies of those for whose death they are personally responsible. My ideas of fighting were all of hand-to-hand encounters—the kind of bloody fighting that rejoiced the hearts of pirates. I considered that it took a brutal kind of man to do such work. For myself I felt certain that, though I got the upper-hand of a fellow who had tried to murder me, I should never have the callousness to return the compliment. The thought of shedding blood was nauseating.

It was partly to escape from this atmosphere of tension that we left London, and set out on a motor-trip through England. This trip had figured largely in our original plans before there had been any thought of war. We wanted to re-visit the old places that had been the scenes of our family-life and childhood. Months before sailing out of Quebec we had studied guidebooks, mapping out routes and hotels. With about half a ton of gasolene on the roof to guard against contingencies, we started.

Everywhere we went, from Cornwall to the North, men were training and marching. All the bridges and reservoirs were guarded. Every tiniest village had its recruiting posters for Kitchener's Army. It was a trip utterly different from the one we had expected.

At Stratford in the tap-room of Shakespeare's favourite tavern I met an exceptional person—a man who was afraid, and had the courage to speak the truth as millions at that time felt it. An American was present—a vast and fleshy man: a transatlantic version of Falstaff. He had just escaped from Paris and was giving us an account of how he had hired a car, had driven as near the fighting-line as he could get and had seen the wounded coming out. He had risked the driver's life and expended large sums of money merely to gratify his curiosity. He mopped his brow and told us that he had aged ten years—folks in Philadelphia would hardly know him; but it was all worth it. The details which he embroidered and dwelt upon were ghastly. He was particularly impressed with having seen a man with his nose off. His description held us horrified and spell-bound.

In the midst of his oratory an officer entered, bringing with him five nervous young fellows. They were self-conscious, excited, over-wrought and belonged to the class of the lawyer's clerk. The officer had evidently been working them up to the point of enlistment, and hoped to complete the job that evening over a sociable glass. As his audience swelled, the fat man from Philadelphia grew exceedingly vivid. When appealed to by the recruiting officer, he confirmed the opinion that every Englishman of fighting age should be in France; that's where the boys of America would be if their country were in the same predicament. Four out of the five intended victims applauded this sentiment—they applauded too boisterously for complete sincerity, because they felt that they could do no less. The fifth, a scholarly, pale-faced fellow, drew attention to himself by his silence.

"You're going to join, too, aren't you?" the recruiting officer asked.

The pale-faced man swallowed. There was no doubt that he was scared. The American's morbid details had been enough to frighten anybody. He was so frightened that he had the pluck to tell the truth.

"I'd like to," he hesitated, "but — —. I've got an imagination. I should see things as twice as horrible. I should live through every beastliness before it occurred. When it did happen, I should turn coward. I should run away, and you'd shoot me as a deserter. I'd like—not yet, I can't."

He was the bravest man in the tap-room that night. If he's still alive, he probably wears decorations. He was afraid, just as every one else was afraid; but he wasn't sufficiently a coward to lie about his terror. His voice was the voice of millions at that hour.

A day came when England's jeopardy was brought home to her. I don't remember the date, but I remember it was a Sabbath. We had pulled up before a village post office to get the news; it was pasted behind the window against the glass. We read, "Boulogne has fallen." The news was false; but it wasn't contradicted till next day. Meanwhile, in that quiet village, over and above the purring of the engine, we heard the beat of Death's wings across the Channel—a gigantic vulture approaching which would pick clean of vileness the bones of both the actually and the spiritually dead. I knew then for certain that it was only a matter of time till I, too, should be out there among the carnage, "somewhere in France." I felt like a rabbit in the last of the standing corn, when a field is in the harvesting. There was no escape—I could hear the scythes of an inexorable duty cutting closer.

After about six weeks in England, I travelled back to New York with my family to complete certain financial obligations and to set about the winding up of my affairs. I said nothing to any one as to my purpose. The reason for my silence is now obvious: I didn't want to commit myself to other people and wished to leave myself a loop-hole for retracting the promises I had made my conscience. There were times when my heart seemed to stop beating, appalled by the future which I was rapidly approaching. My vivid imagination—which from childhood has been as much a hindrance as a help—made me foresee myself in every situation of horror—gassed, broken, distributed over the landscape. Luckily it made me foresee the worst horror—the ignominy of living perhaps fifty years with a self who was dishonoured and had sunk beneath his own best standards. Of course there were also moments of exaltation when the boy-spirit of adventure loomed large; it seemed splendidly absurd that I was going to be a soldier, a companion-in-arms of those lordly chaps who had fought at Senlac, sailed with Drake and saved the day for freedom at Mons. Whether I was exalted or depressed, a power stronger than myself urged me to work feverishly to the end that, at the first opportunity, I might lay aside my occupation, with all my civilian obligations discharged.

When that time came, my first difficulty was in communicating my decision to my family; my second, in getting accepted in Canada. I was perhaps more ignorant than most people about things military. I had not the slightest knowledge as to the functions of the different arms of the service; infantry, artillery, engineers, A.S.C.—they all connoted just as much and as little. I had no qualifications. I had never handled fire-arms. My solitary useful accomplishment was that I could ride a horse. It seemed to me that no man ever was less fitted for the profession of killing. I was painfully conscious of self-ridicule whenever I offered myself for the job. I offered myself several times and in different quarters; when at last I was granted a commission in the Canadian Field Artillery it was by pure good-fortune. I didn't even know what guns were used and, if informed, shouldn't have had the least idea what an eighteen-pounder was. Nevertheless, within seven months I was out in France, taking part in an offensive which, up to that time, was the most ambitious of the entire war.

From New York I went to Kingston in Ontario to present myself for training; an officers' class had just started, in which I had been ordered to enrol myself. It was the depth of winter—an unusually hard winter even for that part of Canada. My first glimpse of the Tête du Pont Barracks was of a square of low buildings, very much like the square of a Hudson Bay Fort. The parade ground was ankle-deep in trampled snow and mud. A bleak wind was blowing from off the river. Squads of embryo officers were being drilled by hoarse-voiced sergeants. The officers looked cold, and cowed, and foolish; the sergeants employed ruthlessly the age-old army sarcasms and made no effort to disguise their disgust for these officers and "temporary gentlemen."

I was directed to an office where a captain sat writing at a desk, while an orderly waited rigidly at attention. The captain looked up as I entered, took in my spats and velour hat with an impatient glance, and continued with his writing. When I got an opportunity I presented my letter; he read it through irritably.

"Any previous military experience?"

"None at all."

"Then how d'you expect to pass out with this class? It's been going for nearly two weeks already?"

Again, as though he had dismissed me from his mind, he returned to his writing. From a military standpoint I knew that I was justly a figure of naught; but I also felt that he was rubbing it in a trifle hard. I was too recent a recruit to have lost my civilian self-respect. At last, after a period of embarrassed silence, I asked, "What am I to do? To whom do I report?"

Without looking up he told me to report on the parade ground at six o'clock the following morning. When I got back to my hotel, I reflected on the chilliness of my reception. I had taken no credit to myself for enlisting—I knew that I ought to have joined months before. But six o'clock! I glanced across at the station, where trains were pulling out for New York; for a moment I was tempted. But not for long; I couldn't trust the hotel people to wake me, so I went out and purchased an alarm clock.

That night I didn't sleep much. I was up and dressed by five-thirty. I hid beneath the shadow of a wall near the barracks and struck matches to look at my watch. At ten minutes to six the street was full of unseen, hurrying feet which sounded ghostly in the darkness. I followed them into the parade-ground. The parade was falling in, rolls were being called by the aid of flash-lamps. I caught hold of an officer; for all I knew he might have been a General or Colonel. I asked his advice, when I had blundered out my story. He laughed and said I had better return to my hotel; the class was going to stables and there was no one at that hour to whom I could report.

The words of the sergeant at the Empire came back to me, "And I'll give you hell if I get you in my squad." I understood then: this was the first attempt of the Army to break my heart—an attempt often repeated and an attempt for which, from my present point of vantage, I am intensely grateful. In those days the Canadian Overseas Forces were comprised of volunteers; it wasn't sufficient to express a tepid willingness to die for your country—you had to prove yourself determined and eligible for death through your power to endure hardship.

When I had been medically examined, passed as fit, had donned a uniform and commenced my training, I learnt what the enduring of hardship was. No experience on active service has equalled the humiliation and severity of those first months of soldiering. We were sneered at, cleaned stables, groomed horses, rode stripped saddle for twelve miles at the trot, attended lectures, studied till past midnight and were up on first parade at six o'clock. No previous civilian efficiency or prominence stood us in any stead. We started robbed of all importance, and only gained a new importance by our power to hang on and to develop a new efficiency as soldiers. When men "went sick" they were labelled scrimshankers and struck off the course. It was an offence to let your body interfere with your duty; if it tried to, you must ignore it. If a man caught cold in Kingston, what would he not catch in the trenches? Very many went down under the physical ordeal; of the class that started, I don't think more than a third passed. The lukewarm soldier and the pink-tea hero, who simply wanted to swank in a uniform, were effectually choked off. It was a test of pluck, even more than of strength or intelligence—the same test that a man would be subjected to all the time at the Front. In a word it sorted out the fellows who had "guts."

"Guts" isn't a particularly polite word, but I have come increasingly to appreciate its splendid significance. The possessor of this much coveted quality is the kind of idiot who,

  "When his legs are smitten off

   Will fight upon his stumps."

The Tommies, whom we were going to command, would be like that; if we weren't like it, we wouldn't be any good as officers. This Artillery School had a violent way of sifting out a man's moral worth; you hadn't much conceit left by the end of it. I had not felt myself so paltry since the day when I was left at my first boarding-school in knickerbockers.

After one had qualified and been appointed to a battery, there was still difficulty in getting to England. I was lucky, and went over early with a draft of officers who had been cabled for as reinforcements. I had been in England a bare three weeks when my name was posted as due to go to France.

How did I feel? Nervous, of course, but also intensely eager. I may have been afraid of wounds and death—I don't remember; I was certainly nothing like as afraid as I had been before I wore uniform. My chief fear was that I would be afraid and might show it. Like the pale-faced chap in the tap-room at Stratford, I had fleeting glimpses of myself being shot as a deserter.

At this point something happened which at least proved to me that I had made moral progress. I'd finished my packing and was doing a last rush round, when I caught in large lettering on a newsboard the heading, "PEACE RUMOURED." Before I realised what had happened I was crying. I was furious with disappointment. If the war should end before I got there—! On buying a paper I assured myself that such a disaster was quite improbable. I breathed again. Then the reproachful memory came of another occasion when I had been scared by a headline, "Boulogne Has Fallen." I had been scared lest I might be needed at that time; now I was panic-stricken lest I might arrive too late. There was a change in me; something deep-rooted had happened. I got to thinking about it. On that motor-trip through England I had considered myself in the light of a philanthropist, who might come to the help of the Allies and might not. Now all I asked was to be considered worthy to do my infinitesimal "bit." I had lost all my old conceits and hallucinations, and had come to respect myself in a very humble fashion not for what I was, but for the cause in which I was prepared to fight. The knowledge that I belonged to the physically fit contributed to this saner sense of pride; before I wore a uniform I had had the morbid fear that I might not be up to standard. And then the uniform! It was the outward symbol of the lost selfishness and the cleaner honour. It hadn't been paid for; it wouldn't be paid for till I had lived in the trenches. I was childishly anxious to earn my right to wear it. I had said "Good-bye" to myself, and had been re-born into willing sacrifice. I think that was the reason for the difference of spirit in which I read the two headlines. We've all gone through the same spiritual gradations, we men who have got to the Front. None of us know how to express our conversion. All we know is that from being little circumscribed egoists, we have swamped our identities in a magnanimous crusade. The venture looked fatal at first; but in losing the whole world we have gained our own souls.

On a beautiful day in late summer I sailed for France. England faded out like a dream behind. Through the haze in mid-Channel a hospital ship came racing; on her sides were blazoned the scarlet cross. The next time I came to England I might travel on that racing ship. The truth sounded like a lie. It seemed far more true that I was going on my annual pleasure trip to the lazy cities of romance.

The port at which we disembarked was cheery and almost normal. One saw a lot of khaki mingling with sky-blue tiger-men of France. Apart from that one would scarcely have guessed that the greatest war in the world's history was raging not more than fifty miles away. I slept the night at a comfortable hotel on the quayside. There was no apparent shortage; I got everything that I required. Next day I boarded a train which, I was told, would carry me to the Front. We puffed along in a leisurely sort of way. The engineer seemed to halt whenever he had a mind; no matter where he halted, grubby children miraculously appeared and ran along the bank, demanding from Monsieur Engleeshman "ceegarettes" and "beescuits." Towards evening we pulled up at a little town where we had a most excellent meal. No hint of war yet. Night came down and we found that our carriage had no lights. It must have been nearing dawn, when I was wakened by the distant thunder of guns. I crouched in my corner, cold and cramped, trying to visualise the terror of it. I asked myself whether I was afraid. "Not of Death," I told myself. "But of being afraid—yes, most horribly."

At five o'clock we halted at a junction, where a troop-train from the Front was already at a standstill. Tommies in steel helmets and muddied to the eyes were swarming out onto the tracks. They looked terrible men with their tanned cheeks and haggard eyes. I felt how impractical I was as I watched them—how ill-suited for campaigning. They were making the most of their respite from travelling. Some were building little fires between the ties to do their cooking—their utensils were bayonets and old tomato cans; others were collecting water from the exhaust of an engine and shaving. I had already tried to purchase food and had failed, so I copied their example and set about shaving.

Later in the day we passed gangs of Hun prisoners—clumsy looking fellows, with flaxen hair and blue eyes, who seemed to be thanking God every minute with smiles that they were out of danger and on our side of the line. Late in the afternoon the engine jumped the rails; we were advised to wander off to a rest-camp, the direction of which was sketchily indicated. We found some Australians with a transport-wagon and persuaded them to help us with our baggage. It had been pouring heavily, but the clouds had dispersed and a rainbow spanned the sky. I took it for a sign.

After trudging about six miles, we arrived at the camp and found that it was out of food and that all the tents were occupied. We stretched our sleeping-bags on the ground and went to bed supperless. We had had no food all day. Next morning we were told that we ought to jump an ammunition-lorry, if we wanted to get any further on our journey. Nobody seemed to want us particularly, and no one could give us the least information as to where our division was. It was another lesson, if that were needed, of our total unimportance. While we were waiting on the roadside, an Australian brigade of artillery passed by. The men's faces were dreary with fatigue; the gunners were dismounted and marched as in a trance. The harness was muddy, the steel rusty, the horses lean and discouraged. We understood that they were pulling out from an offensive in which they had received a bad cutting up. To my overstrained imagination it seemed that the men had the vision of death in their eyes.

Presently we spotted a lorry-driver who had, what George Robey would call, "a kind and generous face." We took advantage of him, for once having persuaded him to give us a lift, we froze onto him and made him cart us about the country all day. We kept him kind and generous, I regret to say, by buying him wine at far too many estaminets.

Towards evening the thunder of the guns had swelled into an ominous roar. We passed through villages disfigured by shell-fire. Civilians became more rare and more aged. Cattle disappeared utterly from the landscape; fields were furrowed with abandoned trenches, in front of which hung entanglements of wire. Mounted orderlies splashed along sullen roads at an impatient trot. Here and there we came across improvised bivouacs of infantry. Far away against the horizon towards which we travelled, Hun flares and rockets were going up. Hopeless stoicism, unutterable desolation—that was my first impression.

The landscape was getting increasingly muddy—it became a sea of mud. Despatch-riders on motor-bikes travelled warily, with their feet dragging to save themselves from falling. Everything was splashed with filth and corruption; one marvelled at the cleanness of the sky. Trees were blasted, and seemed to be sinking out of sight in this war-created Slough of

Despond. We came to the brow of a hill; in the valley was something that I recognised. The last time I had seen it was in an etching in a shop window in Newark, New Jersey. It was a town, from the midst of whose battered ruins a splintered tower soared against the sky. Leaning far out from the tower, so that it seemed she must drop, was a statue of the Virgin with the Christ in her arms. It was a superstition with the French, I remembered, that so long as she did not fall, things would go well with the Allies. As we watched, a shell screamed over the gaping roofs and a column of smoke went up. Gehenna, being blessed by the infant Jesus — that was what I saw.

As we entered the streets, Tommies more polluted than miners crept out from the skeletons of houses. They leant listlessly against sagging doorways to watch us pass. If we asked for information as to where our division was, they shook their heads stupidly, too indifferent with weariness to reply. We found the Town Mayor; all that he could tell us was that our division wasn't here yet, but was expected any day — probably it was still on the line of march. Our lorry-driver was growing impatient. We wrote him out a note which would explain his wanderings, got him to deposit us near a Y. M. C. A. tent, and bade him an uncordial "Good-bye." For the next three nights we slept by our wits and got our food by foraging.

There was a Headquarters near by whose battalion was in the line. I struck up a liaison with its officers, and at times went into the crowded tent, which was their mess, to get warm. Runners would come there at all hours of the day and night, bringing messages from the Front. They were usually well spent. Sometimes they had been gassed; but they all had the invincible determination to carry on. After they had delivered their message, they would lie down in the mud and go to sleep like dogs. The moment the reply was ready, they would lurch to their feet, throwing off their weariness, as though it were a thing to be conquered and despised. I appreciated now, as never before, the lesson of "guts" that I had been taught at Kingston.

There was one officer at Battalion Headquarters who, whenever I entered, was always writing, writing, writing. What he was writing I never enquired — perhaps letters to his sweetheart or wife. It didn't matter how long I stayed, he never seemed to have the time to look up. He was a Highlander—a big man with a look of fate in his eyes. His hair was black; his face stern, and set, and extremely white. I remember once seeing him long after midnight through the raised flap of the tent. All his brother officers were asleep, huddled like sacks impersonally on the floor. At the table in the centre he sat, his head bowed in his hands, the light from the lamp spilling over his neck and forehead. He may have been praying. He recalled to my mind the famous picture of The Last Sleep of Argyle. From that moment I had the premonition that he would not live long. A month later I learnt that he had been killed on his next trip into the trenches.

After three days of waiting my division arrived and I was attached to a battery. I had scarcely had time to make the acquaintance of my new companions, when we pulled into my first attack.

We hooked in at dawn and set out through a dense white mist. The mist was wet and miserable, but excellent for our purpose; it prevented us from being spotted by enemy balloons and aeroplanes. We made all the haste that was possible; but in places the roads were blocked by other batteries moving into new positions. We passed through the town above which the Virgin floated with the infant Jesus in her arms. One wondered whether she was really holding him out to bless; her attitude might equally have been that of one who was flinging him down into the shambles, disgusted with this travesty on religion.

The other side of the town the ravages of war were far more marked. All the way along the roadside were clumps of little crosses, French, English, German, planted above the hurried graves of the brave fellows who had fallen. Ambulances were picking their way warily, returning with the last night's toll of wounded. We saw newly dead men and horses, pulled to one side, who had been caught in the darkness by the enemy's harassing fire. In places the country had holes the size of quarries, where mines had exploded and shells from large calibre guns had detonated. Bedlam was raging up front; shells went screaming over us, seeking out victims in the back-country. To have been there by oneself would have been most disturbing, but the men about me seemed to regard it as perfectly ordinary and normal. I steadied myself by their example.

We came to a point where our Major was waiting for us, turned out of the road, followed him down a grass slope and so into a valley. Here gun-pits were in the process of construction. Guns were unhooked and man-handled into their positions, and the teams sent back to the wagon-lines. All day we worked, both officers and men, with pick and shovel. Towards evening we had completed the gun-platforms and made a beginning on the overhead cover. We had had no time to prepare sleeping-quarters, so spread our sleeping-bags and blankets in the caved-in trenches. About seven o'clock, as we were resting, the evening "hate" commenced. In those days the evening "hate" was a regular habit with the Hun. He knew our country better than we did, for he had retired from it. Every evening he used to search out all communication trenches and likely battery-positions with any quantity of shells. His idea was to rob us of our morale. I wish he might have seen how abysmally he failed to do it. Down our narrow valley, like a flight of arrows, the shells screamed and whistled. Where they struck, the ground looked like Resurrection Day with the dead elbowing their way into daylight and forcing back the earth from their eyes. There were actually many dead just beneath the surface and, as the ground was ploughed up, the smell of corruption became distinctly unpleasant. Presently the shells began to go dud; we realised that they were gas-shells. A thin, bluish vapour spread throughout the valley and breathing became oppressive. Then like stallions, kicking in their stalls, the heavy guns on the ridge above us opened. It was fine to hear them stamping their defiance; it made one want to get to grips with his aggressors. In the brief silences one could hear our chaps laughing. The danger seemed to fill them with a wild excitement. Every time a shell came near and missed them, they would taunt the unseen Huns for their poor gunnery, giving what they considered the necessary corrections: "Five minutes more left, old Cock. If you'd only drop fifty, you'd get us." These men didn't know what fear was—or, if they did, they kept it to themselves. And these were the chaps whom I was to order.

A few days later my Major told me that I was to be ready at 3:30 next morning to accompany him up front to register the guns. In registering guns you take a telephonist and linesmen with you. They lay in a line from the battery to any point you may select as the best from which to observe the enemy's country. This point may be two miles or more in advance of your battery. Your battery is always hidden and out of sight, for fear the enemy should see the flash of the firing; consequently the officer in charge of the battery lays the guns mathematically, but cannot observe the effect of his shots. The officer who goes forward can see the target; by telephoning back his corrections, he makes himself the eyes of the officer at the guns.

It had been raining when we crept out of our kennels to go forward. It seems unnecessary to state that it had been raining, for it always has been raining at the Front. I don't remember what degree of mud we had attained. We have a variety of adjectives, and none of them polite, to describe each stage. The worst of all is what we call "God-Awful Mud." I don't think it was as bad as that, but it was bad enough. Everything was dim, and clammy, and spectral. At the hour of dawn one isn't at his bravest. It was like walking at the bottom of the sea, only things that were thrown at you travelled faster. We struck a sloppy road, along which ghostly figures passed, with ground sheets flung across their head and shoulders, like hooded monks. At a point where scarlet bundles were being lifted into ambulances, we branched overland. Here and there from all directions, infantry were converging, picking their way in single file to reduce their casualties if a shell burst near them. The landscape, the people, the early morning—everything was stealthy and walked with muted steps.

We entered a trench. Holes were scooped out in the side of it just large enough to shelter a man crouching. Each hole contained a sleeping soldier who looked as dead as the occupant of a catacomb. Some of the holes had been blown in; all you saw of the late occupant was a protruding arm or leg. At best there was a horrid similarity between the dead and the living. It seemed that the walls of the trenches had been built out of corpses, for one recognised the uniforms of French men and Huns. They were built out of them, though whether by design or accident it was impossible to tell. We came to a group of men, doing some repairing; that part of the trench had evidently been strafed last night. They didn't know where they were, or how far it was to the front-line. We wandered on, still laying in our wire. The Colonel of our Brigade joined us and we waded on together.

The enemy shelling was growing more intense, as was always the way on the Somme when we were bringing out our wounded. A good many of our trenches were directly enfilade; shells burst just behind the parapet, when they didn't burst on it. It was at about this point in my breaking-in that I received a blow on the head—and thanked God for the man who invented the steel helmet.

Things were getting distinctly curious. We hadn't passed any infantry for some time. The trenches were becoming each minute more shallow and neglected. Suddenly we found ourselves in a narrow furrow which was packed with our own dead. They had been there for some time and were partly buried. They were sitting up or lying forward in every attitude of agony. Some of them clasped their wounds; some of them pointed with their hands. Their faces had changed to every colour and glared at us like swollen bruises. Their helmets were off; with a pitiful, derisive neatness the rain had parted their hair.

We had to crouch low because the trench was so shallow. It was difficult not to disturb them; the long skirts of our trench-coats brushed against their faces.

All of a sudden we halted, making ourselves as small as could be. In the rapidly thinning mist ahead of us, men were moving. They were stretcher-bearers. The odd thing was that they were carrying their wounded away from, instead of towards us. Then it flashed on us that they were Huns. We had wandered into No Man's Land. Almost at that moment we must have been spotted, for shells commenced falling at the end of the trench by which we had entered. Spreading out, so as not to attract attention, we commenced to crawl towards the other end. Instantly that also was closed to us and a curtain of shells started dropping behind us. We were trapped. With perfect coolness—a coolness which, whatever I looked, I did not share—we went down on our hands and knees, wriggling our way through the corpses and shell-holes in the direction of where our front-line ought to be. After what seemed an age, we got back. Later we registered the guns, and one of our officers who had been laying in wire, was killed in the process. His death, like everything else, was regarded without emotion as being quite ordinary.

On the way out, when we had come to a part of our journey where the tension was relaxed and we could be less cautious, I saw a signalling officer lying asleep under a blackened tree. I called my Major's attention to him, saying, "Look at that silly ass, sir. He'll get something that he doesn't want if he lies there much longer."

My Major turned his head, and said briefly, "Poor chap, he's got it."

Then I saw that his shoulder-blade had burst through his tunic and was protruding. He'd been coming out, walking freely and feeling that the danger was over, just as we were, when the unlucky shell had caught him. "His name must have been written on it," our men say when that happens. I noticed that he had black boots; since then nothing would persuade me to wear black boots in the trenches.

This first experience in No Man's Land did away with my last flabby fear — that, if I was afraid, I would show it. One is often afraid. Any soldier who asserts the contrary may not be a liar, but he certainly does not speak the truth. Physical fear is too deeply rooted to be overcome by any amount of training; it remains, then, to train a man in spiritual pride, so that when he fears, nobody knows it. Cowardice is contagious. It has been said that no battalion is braver than its least brave member. Military courage is, therefore, a form of unselfishness; it is practised that it may save weaker men's lives and uphold their honour. The worst thing you can say of a man at the Front is, "He doesn't play the game." That doesn't of necessity mean that he fails to do his duty; what it means is that he fails to do a little bit more than his duty.

When a man plays the game, he does things which it requires a braver man than himself to accomplish; he never knows when he's done; he acknowledges no limit to his cheerfulness and strength; whatever his rank, he holds his life less valuable than that of the humblest; he laughs at danger not because he does not dread it, but because he has learnt that there are ailments more terrible and less curable than death.

The men in the ranks taught me whatever I know about playing the game. I learnt from their example. In acknowledging this, I own up to the new equality, based on heroic values, which this war has established. The only man who counts "out there" is the man who is sufficiently self-effacing to show courage. The chaps who haven't done it are the exceptions.

At the start of the war there were a good many persons whom we were apt to think of as common and unclean. But social distinctions are a wash-out in the trenches. We have seen St. Peter's vision, and have heard the voice, "What God hath cleansed, that call not thou common."

Until I became a part of the war, I was a doubter of nobility in others and a sceptic as regards myself. The growth of my personal vision was complete when I recognised that the capacity of heroism is latent in everybody, and only awaits the bigness of the opportunity to call it out.

THE GLORY OF THE TRENCHES

We were too proud to live for years

When our poor death could dry the tears

Of little children yet unborn.

It scarcely mattered that at morn,

When manhood's hope was at its height,

We stopped a bullet in mid-flight.

It did not trouble us to lie

Forgotten 'neath the forgetting sky.

So long Sleep was our only cure

That when Death piped of rest made sure,

We cast our fleshly crutches down,

Laughing like boys in Hamelin Town.

And this we did while loving life,

Yet loving more than home or wife

The kindness of a world set free

For countless children yet to be.

III. GOD AS WE SEE HIM

For some time before I was wounded, we had been in very hot places. We could scarcely expect them to be otherwise, for we had put on show after show. A "show" in our language, I should explain, has nothing in common with a theatrical performance, though it does not lack drama. We make the term apply to any method of irritating the Hun, from a trench-raid to a big offensive. The Hun was decidedly annoyed. He had very good reason. We were occupying the dug-outs which he had spent two years in building with French civilian labour. His U-boat threats had failed. He had offered us the olive-branch, and his peace terms had been rejected with a peal of guns all along the Western Front. He had shown his disapproval of us by paying particular attention to our batteries; as a consequence our shell-dressings were all used up, having gone out with the gentlemen on stretchers who were contemplating a vacation in Blighty. We couldn't get enough to re-place them. There was a hitch somewhere. The demand for shell-dressings exceeded the supply. So I got on my horse one Sunday and, with my groom accompanying me, rode into the back-country to see if I couldn't pick some up at various Field Dressing Stations and Collecting Points.

In the course of my wanderings I came to a cathedral city. It was a city which was and still is beautiful, despite the constant bombardments. The Huns had just finished hurling a few more tons of explosives into it as I and my groom entered. The streets were deserted; it might have been a city of the dead. There was no sound, except the ringing iron of our horses' shoes on the cobble pavement. Here and there we came to what looked like a barricade which barred our progress; actually it was the piled-up walls and rubbish of buildings which had collapsed. From cellars, now and then, faces of women, children and ancient men peered out—they were sharp and pointed like rats. One's imagination went back five hundred years—everything seemed mediaeval, short-lived and brutal. This might have been Limoges after the Black Prince had finished massacring its citizens; or it might have been Paris, when the wolves came down and François Villon tried to find a lodging for the night.

I turned up through narrow alleys where grass was growing and found myself, almost by accident, in a garden. It was a green and spacious garden, with fifteen-foot walls about it and flowers which scattered themselves broadcast in neglected riot. We dismounted and tied our horses. Wandering along its paths, we came across little summer-houses, statues, fountains and then, without any hindrance, found ourselves in the nave of a fine cathedral which was roofed only by the sky. Two years of the Huns had made it as much a ruin as Tintern Abbey. Here, too, the flowers had intruded. They grew between graves in the pavement and scrambled up the walls, wherever they could find a foothold. At the far end of this stretch of destruction stood the high altar, totally untouched by the hurricane of shell-fire. The saints were perched in their niches, composed and stately. The Christ looked down from His cross, as he had done for centuries, sweeping the length of splendid architecture with sad eyes. It seemed a miracle that the altar had been spared, when everything else had fallen. A reason is given for its escape. Every Sabbath since the start of the war, no matter how severe the bombardment, service has been held there. The thin-faced women, rat-faced children and ancient men have crept out from their cellars and gathered about the priest; the lamp has been lit, the Host uplifted. The Hun is aware of this; with malice aforethought he lands shells into the cathedral every Sunday in an effort to smash the altar. So far he has failed. One finds in this a symbol — that in the heart of the maelstrom of horror, which this war has created, there is a quiet place where the lamp of gentleness and honour is kept burning. The Hun will have to do a lot more shelling before he puts the lamp of kindness out. From the polluted trenches of Vimy the poppies spring up, blazoning abroad in vivid scarlet the heroism of our lads' willing sacrifice. All this April, high above the shouting of our guns, the larks sang joyously. The scarlet of the poppies, the song of the larks, the lamp shining on the altar are only external signs of the unconquerable, happy religion which lies hidden in the hearts of our men. Their religion is the religion of heroism, which they have learnt in the glory of the trenches.

There was a line from William Morris's Earthly Paradise which used to haunt me, especially in the early days when I was first experiencing what war really meant. Since returning for a brief space to where books are accessible, I have looked up the quotation. It reads as follows: —

"Of Heaven or Hell I have no power to sing,

I cannot ease the burden of your fears

Or make quick-coming death a little thing."

It is the last line that makes me smile rather quietly, "Or make quick-coming death a little thing." I smile because the souls who wear khaki have learnt to do just that. Morris goes on to say that all he can do to make people happy is to tell them deathless stories about heroes who have passed into the world of the imagination, and, because of that, are immune from death. He calls himself "the idle singer of an empty day." How typical he is of the days before the war when people had only pin-pricks to endure, and, consequently, didn't exert themselves to be brave! A big sacrifice, which bankrupts one's life, is always more bearable than the little inevitable annoyances of sickness, disappointment and dying in a bed. It's easier for Christ to go to Calvary than for an on-looker to lose a night's sleep in the garden. When the world went well with us before the war, we were doubters. Nearly all the fiction of the past fifteen years is a proof of that—it records our fear of failure, sex, old age and particularly of a God who refuses to explain Himself. Now, when we have thrust the world, affections, life itself behind us and gaze hourly into the eyes of Death, belief comes as simply and clearly as it did when we were children. Curious and extraordinary! The burden of our fears has slipped from our shoulders in our attempt to do something for others; the unbelievable and long coveted miracle has happened—at last to every soul who has grasped his chance of heroism quick-coming death has become a fifth-rate calamity.

In saying this I do not mean to glorify war; war can never be anything but beastly and damnable. It dates back to the jungle. But there are two kinds of war. There's the kind that a highwayman wages, when he pounces from the bushes and assaults a defenceless woman; there's the kind you wage when you go to her rescue. The highwayman can't expect to come out of the fight with a loftier morality—you can. Our chaps never wanted to fight. They hate fighting; it's that hatred of the thing they are compelled to do that makes them so terrible. The last thought to enter their heads four years ago was that to-day they would be in khaki. They had never been trained to the use of arms; a good many of them conceived of themselves as cowards. They entered the war to defend rather than to destroy. They literally put behind them houses, brethren, sisters, father, mother, wife, children, lands for the Kingdom of Heaven's sake, though they would be the last to express themselves in that fashion.

At a cross-road at the bottom of a hill, on the way to a gun-position we once had, stood a Calvary—one of those wayside altars, so frequently met in France, with pollarded trees surrounding it and an image of Christ in His agony. Pious peasants on their journey to market or as they worked in the fields, had been accustomed to raise their eyes to it and cross themselves. It had comforted them with the knowledge of protection. The road leading back from it and up the hill was gleaming white—a direct enfilade for the Hun, and always under observation. He kept guns trained on it; at odd intervals, any hour during the day or night, he would sweep it with shell-fire. The woods in the vicinity were blasted and blackened. It was the season for leaves and flowers, but there was no greenness. Whatever of vegetation had not been uprooted and buried, had been poisoned by gas. The atmosphere was vile with the odour of decaying flesh. In the early morning, if you passed by the Calvary, there was always some fresh tragedy. The newly dead lay sprawled out against its steps, as though they had dragged themselves there in their last moments. If you looked along the road, all the glazed eyes seemed to stare towards it. "Lord, remember me when thou comest into thy Kingdom," they seemed to say. The wooden Christ gazed down on them from His cross, with a suffering which two thousand years ago he had shared. The terrible pity of His silence seemed to be telling them that they had become one with Him in their final sacrifice. They hadn't lived His life—far from it; unknowingly they had died His death. That's a part of the glory of the trenches, that a man who has not been good, can crucify himself and hang beside Christ in the end. One wonders in what pleasant places those weary souls find rest.

There was a second Calvary—a heap of ruins. Nothing of the altar or trees, by which it had been surrounded, was left. The first time I passed it, I saw a foot protruding. The man might be wounded; I climbed up to examine and pulled aside the debris. Beneath it I found, like that of one three weeks dead, the naked body of the Christ. The exploding shell had wrenched it from its cross. Aslant the face, with gratuitous blasphemy, the crown of thorns was tilted.

These two Calvaries picture for me the part that Christ is playing in the present war. He survives in the noble self-effacement of the men. He is re-crucified in the defilements that are wrought upon their bodies.

God as we see Him! And do we see Him? I think so, but not always consciously. He moves among us in the forms of our brother men. We see him most evidently when danger is most threatening and courage is at its highest. We don't often recognise Him out loud. Our chaps don't assert that they're His fellow-campaigners. They're too humble-minded and inarticulate for that. They're where they are because they want to do their "bit"—their duty. A carefully disguised instinct of honour brought them there. "Doing their bit" in Bible language means, laying down their lives for their friends. After all they're not so far from Nazareth.

"Doing their bit!" That covers everything. Here's an example of how God walks among us. In one of our attacks on the Somme, all the observers up forward were uncertain as to what had happened. We didn't know whether our infantry had captured their objective, failed, or gone beyond it. The battlefield, as far as eye could reach, was a bath of mud. It is extremely easy in the excitement of an offensive, when all landmarks are blotted out, for our storming parties to lose their direction. If this happens, a number of dangers may result. A battalion may find itself "up in the air," which means that it has failed to connect with the battalions on its right and left; its flanks are then exposed to the enemy. It may advance too far, and start digging itself in at a point where it was previously arranged that our artillery should place their protective wall of fire. We, being up forward as artillery observers, are the eyes of the army. It is our business to watch for such contingencies, to keep in touch with the situation as it progresses and to send our information back as quickly as possible. We were peering through our glasses from our point of vantage when, far away in the thickest of the battle-smoke, we saw a white flag wagging, sending back messages. The flag-wagging was repeated desperately; it was evident that no one had replied, and probable that no one had picked up the messages. A signaller who was with us, read the language for us. A company of infantry had advanced too far; they were most of them wounded, very many of them dead, and they were in danger of being surrounded. They asked for our artillery to place a curtain of fire in front of them, and for reinforcements to be sent up.

We at once 'phoned the orders through to our artillery and notified the infantry headquarters of the division that was holding that front. But it was necessary to let those chaps know that we were aware of their predicament. They'd hang on if they knew that; otherwise — —.

Without orders our signaller was getting his flags ready. If he hopped out of the trench onto the parapet, he didn't stand a fifty-fifty chance. The Hun was familiar with our observation station and strafed it with persistent regularity.

The signaller turned to the senior officer present, "What will I send them, sir?"

"Tell them their messages have been received and that help is coming."

Out the chap scrambled, a flag in either hand — he was nothing but a boy. He ran crouching like a rabbit to a hump of mud where his figure would show up against the sky. His flags commenced wagging, "Messages received. Help coming." They didn't see him at first. He had to repeat the words. We watched him breathlessly. We knew what would happen; at last it happened. A Hun observer had spotted him and flashed the target back to his guns. All about him the mud commenced to leap and bubble. He went on signalling the good word to those stranded men up front, "Messages received. Help coming." At last they'd seen him. They were signaling, "O. K." It was at that moment that a whizz-bang lifted him off his feet and landed him all of a huddle. His "bit!" It was what he'd volunteered to do, when he came from Canada. The signalled "O. K." in the battlesmoke was like a testimony to his character.

That's the kind of peep at God we get on the Western Front. It isn't a sad peep, either. When men die for something worth while death loses all its terror. It's petering out in bed from sickness or old age that's so horrifying. Many a man, whose cowardice is at loggerheads with his sense of duty, comes to the Front as a non-combatant; he compromises with his conscience and takes a bomb-proof job in some service whose place is well behind the lines. He doesn't stop there long, if he's a decent sort. Having learnt more than ever he guessed before about the brutal things that shell-fire can do to you, he transfers into a fighting unit. Why? Because danger doesn't appal; it allures. It holds a challenge. It stings one's pride. It urges one to seek out ascending scales of risk, just to prove to himself that he isn't flabby. The safe job is the only job for which there's no competition in fighting units. You have to persuade men to be grooms, or cooks, or batmen. If you're seeking volunteers for a chance at annihilation, you have to cast lots to avoid the offence of rejecting. All of this is inexplicable to civilians. I've heard them call the men at the Front "spiritual geniuses"—which sounds splendid, but means nothing.

If civilian philosophers fail to explain us, we can explain them. In their world they are the centre of their universe. They look inward, instead of outward. The sun rises and sets to minister to their particular happiness. If they should die, the stars would vanish. We understand; a few months ago we, too, were like that. What makes us reckless of death is our intense gratitude that we have altered. We want to prove to ourselves in excess how utterly we are changed from what we were. In his secret heart the egotist is a self-despiser. Can you imagine what a difference it works in a man after years of self-contempt, at least for one brief moment to approve of himself? Ever since we can remember, we were chained to the prison-house of our bodies; we lived to feed our bodies, to clothe our bodies, to preserve our bodies, to minister to their passions. Now we know that our bodies are mere flimsy shells, in which our souls are paramount. We can fling them aside any minute; they become ignoble the moment the soul has departed. We have proof. Often at zero hour we have seen whole populations of cities go over the top and vanish, leaving behind them their bloody rags. We should go mad if we did not believe in immortality. We know that the physical is not the essential part. How better can a man shake off his flesh than at the hour when his spirit is most shining? The exact day when he dies does not matter—to-morrow or fifty years hence. The vital concern is not when, but how. The civilian philosopher considers what we've lost. He forgets that it could never have been ours for long. In many cases it was misused and scarcely worth having while it lasted. Some of us were too weak to use it well. We might use it better now. We turn from such thoughts and reckon up our gains. On the debit side we place ourselves as we were. We probably caught a train every morning—the same train, we went to a business where we sat at a desk. Neither the business nor the desk ever altered. We received the same strafing from the same employer; or, if we were the employer, we administered the same strafing. We only did these things that we might eat bread; our dreams were all selfish—of more clothes, more respect, more food, bigger houses. The least part of the day we devoted to the people and the things we really cared for. And the people we loved—we weren't always nice to them. On the credit side we place ourselves as we are—doing a man's job, doing it for some one else, and unafraid to meet God.

Before the war the word "ideals" had grown out-of-date and priggish—we had substituted for it the more robust word "ambitions." Today ideals have come back to their place in our vocabulary. We have forgotten that we ever had ambitions, but at this moment men are drowning for ideals in the mud of Flanders.

Nevertheless, it is true; it isn't natural to be brave. How, then, have multitudes of men acquired this sudden knack of courage? They have been educated by the greatness of the occasion; when big sacrifices have been demanded, men have never been found lacking. And they have acquired it through discipline and training.

When you have subjected yourself to discipline, you cease to think of yourself; you are not you, but a part of a company of men. If you don't do your duty, you throw the whole machine out. You soon learn the hard lesson that every man's life and every man's service belong to other people. Of this the organisation of an army is a vivid illustration. Take the infantry, for instance. They can't fight by themselves; they're dependent on the support of the artillery. The artillery, in their turn, would be terribly crippled, were it not for the gallantry of the air service. If the infantry collapse, the guns have to go back; if the infantry advance, the guns have to be pulled forward. This close interdependence of service on service, division on division, battalion on battery, follows right down through the army till it reaches the individual, so that each man feels that the day will be lost if he fails. His imagination becomes intrigued by the immensity of the stakes for which he plays. Any physical calamity which may happen to himself becomes trifling when compared with the disgrace he would bring upon his regiment if he were not courageous.

A few months ago I was handing over a battery-position in a fairly warm place. The major, who came up to take over from me, brought with him a subaltern and just enough men to run the guns. Within half-an-hour of their arrival, a stray shell came over and caught the subaltern and five of the gun-detachment. It was plain at once that the subaltern was dying — his name must have been written on the shell, as we say in France. We got a stretcher and made all haste to rush him out to a dressing-station. Just as he was leaving, he asked to speak with his major. "I'm so sorry, sir; I didn't mean to get wounded," he whispered. The last word he sent back from the dressing-station where he died, was, "Tell the major, I didn't mean to do it." That's discipline. He didn't think of himself; all he thought of was that his major would be left short-handed.

Here's another story, illustrating how mercilessly discipline can restore a man to his higher self. Last spring, the night before an attack, a man was brought into a battalion headquarters dug-out, under arrest. The adjutant and Colonel were busy attending to the last details of their preparations. The adjutant looked up irritably,

"What is it?"

The N. C. O. of the guard answered, "We found this man, sir, in a communication trench. His company has been in the front-line two hours. He was sitting down, with his equipment thrown away, and evidently had no intention of going up."

The adjutant glanced coldly at the prisoner. "What have you to say for yourself?"

The man was ghastly white and shaking like an aspen. "Sir, I'm not the man I was since I saw my best friend, Jimmie, with his head blown off and lying in his hands. It's kind of got me. I can't face up to it."

The adjutant was silent for a few seconds; then he said, "You know you have a double choice. You can either be shot up there, doing your duty, or behind the lines as a coward. It's for you to choose. I don't care."

The interview was ended. He turned again to the Colonel. The man slowly straightened himself, saluted like a soldier and marched out alone to the Front. That's what discipline does for a man who's going back on himself.

One of the big influences that helps to keep a soldier's soul sanitary is what is known in the British Army as "spit and polish." Directly we pull out for a rest, we start to work burnishing and washing. The chaps may have shown the most brilliant courage and self-sacrificing endurance, it counts for nothing if they're untidy. The first morning, no matter what are the weather conditions, we hold an inspection; every man has to show up with his chin shaved, hair cut, leather polished and buttons shining. If he doesn't he gets hell.

There's a lot in it. You bring a man out from a tight corner where he's been in hourly contact with death; he's apt to think, "What's the use of taking pride in myself. I'm likely to be 'done in' any day. It'll be all the same when I'm dead." But if he doesn't keep clean in his body, he won't keep clean in his mind. The man who has his buttons shining brightly and his leather polished, is usually the man who is brightly polished inside. Spit and polish teaches a man to come out of the trenches from seeing his pals killed, and to carry on as though nothing abnormal had happened. It educates him in an impersonal attitude towards calamity which makes it bearable. It forces him not to regard anything too tragically. If you can stand aside from yourself and poke fun at your own tragedy—and tragedy always has its humorous aspect—that helps. The songs which have been inspired by the trenches are examples of this tendency.

The last thing you find anybody singing "out there" is something patriotic; the last thing you find anybody reading is Rupert Brooke's poems. When men sing among the shell-holes they prefer a song which belittles their own heroism. Please picture to yourself a company of mud-stained scarecrows in steel-helmets, plodding their way under intermittent shelling through a battered trench, whistling and humming the following splendid sentiments from The Plea of The Conscientious Objector: —

"Send us the Army and the Navy. Send us the rank and file.

 Send us the grand old Territorials — they'll face the danger with a smile.

 Where are the boys of the Old Brigade who made old England free?

 You may send my mother, my sister or my brother,

 But for Gawd's sake don't send me."

They leave off whistling and humming to shout the last line. A shell falls near them — then another, then another. They crouch for a minute against the sticky walls to escape the flying spray of death. Then they plod onward again through the mud whistling and humming, "But for Gawd's sake don't send me." They're probably a carrying party, taking up the rations to their pals. It's quite likely they'll have a bad time to-night — there's the smell of gas in the air. Good luck to them. They disappear round the next traverse.

Our men sing many mad burlesques on their own splendour — parodies on their daily fineness. Here's a last example — a take-off on "A Little Bit of Heaven:"

 "Oh a little bit of shrapnel fell from out the sky one day

 And it landed on a soldier in a field not far away;

 But when they went to find him he was bust beyond repair,

 So they pulled his legs and arms off and they left him lying there.

 Then they buried him in Flanders just to make the new crops grow.

 He'll make the best manure, they say, and sure they ought to know.

 And they put a little cross up which bore his name so grand,

 On the day he took his farewell for a better Promised Land."

One learns to laugh — one has to — just as he has to learn to believe in immortality. The Front affords plenty of occasions for humour if a man has only learnt to laugh at himself. I had been sent forward to report at a battalion headquarters as liaison officer for an attack. The headquarters were in a captured dug-out somewhere under a ruined house. Just as I got there and was searching among the fallen walls for an entrance, the Hun barrage came down. It was like the Yellowstone Park when all the geysers are angry at the same time. Roofs, beams, chips of stone commenced to fly in every direction. In the middle of the hubbub a small dump of bombs was struck by a shell and started to explode behind me. The blast of the explosion caught me up and hurled me down fifteen stairs of the dug-out I had been trying to discover. I landed on all fours in a place full of darkness; a door banged behind me. I don't know how long I lay there. Something was squirming under me. A voice said plaintively, "I don't know who you are, but I wish you'd get off. I'm the adjutant."

It's a queer country, that place we call "out there." You approach our front-line, as it is to-day, across anywhere from five to twenty miles of battlefields. Nothing in the way of habitation is left. Everything has been beaten into pulp by hurricanes of shell-fire. First you come to a metropolis of horse-lines, which makes you think that a mammoth circus has arrived. Then you come to plank roads and little light railways, running out like veins across the mud. Far away there's a ridge and a row of charred trees, which stand out gloomily etched against the sky. The sky is grey and damp and sickly; fleecy balls of smoke burst against it—shrapnel. You wonder whether they've caught anybody. Overhead you hear the purr of engines— a flight of aeroplanes breasting the clouds. Behind you observation balloons hang stationary, like gigantic tethered sausages.

If you're riding, you dismount before you reach the ridge and send your horse back; the Hun country is in sight on the other side. You creep up cautiously, taking careful note of where the shells are falling. There's nothing to be gained by walking into a barrage; you make up your mind to wait. The rate of fire has slackened; you make a dash for it. From the ridge there's a pathway which runs down through the blackened wood; two men going alone are not likely to be spotted. Not likely, but—. There's an old cement Hun gun-pit to the right; you take cover in it. "Pretty wide awake," you say to your companion, "to have picked us out as quickly as that."

From this sheltered hiding you have time to gaze about you. The roof of the gun-pit is smashed in at one corner. Our heavies did that when the Hun held the ridge. It was good shooting. A perfect warren of tunnels and dug-outs leads off in every direction. They were built by the forced labour of captive French civilians. We have found requests from them scrawled in pencil on the boards: "I, Jean Ribeau, was alive and well on May 12th, 1915. If this meets the eye of a friend, I beg that he will inform my wife," etc.; after which follows the wife's address. These underground fortifications proved as much a snare as a protection to our enemies. I smile to remember how after our infantry had advanced three miles, they captured a Hun major busily shaving himself in his dug-out, quite unaware that anything unusual was happening. He was very angry because he had been calling in vain for his man to bring his hot water. When he heard the footsteps of our infantry on the stairs, he thought it was his servant and started strafing. He got the surprise of his venerable life when he saw the khaki.

From the gun-pit the hill slants steeply to the plain. It was once finely wooded. Now the trees lie thick as corpses where an attack has failed, scythed down by bursting shells. From the foot of the hill the plain spreads out, a sea of furrowed slime and craters. It's difficult to pick out trenches. Nothing is moving. It's hard to believe that anything can live down there. Suddenly, as though a gigantic egg-beater were at work, the mud is thrashed and tormented. Smoke drifts across the area that is being strafed; through the smoke the stakes and wire hurtle. If you hadn't been in flurries of that sort yourself, you'd think that no one could exist through it. It's ended now; once again the country lies dead and breathless in a kind of horrible suspense. Suspense! Yes, that's the word.

Beyond the mud, in the far cool distance is a green untroubled country. The Huns live there. That's the worst of doing all the attacking; we live on the recent battlefields we have won, whereas the enemy retreats into untouched cleanness. One can see church steeples peeping above woods, chateaus gleaming, and stretches of shining river. It looks innocent and kindly, but from the depth of its greenness invisible eyes peer out. Do you make one unwary movement, and over comes a flock of shells.

At night from out this swamp of vileness a phantom city floats up; it is composed of the white Very lights and multi-coloured flares which the Hun employs to protect his front-line from our patrols. For brief spells No Man's Land becomes brilliant as day. Many of his flares are prearranged signals, meaning that his artillery is shooting short or calling for an S.O.S. The combination of lights which mean these things are changed with great frequency, lest we should guess. The on-looker, with a long night of observing before him, becomes imaginative and weaves out for the dancing lights a kind of Shell-Hole Nights' Entertainment. The phantom city over there is London, New York, Paris, according to his fancy. He's going out to dinner with his girl. All those flares are arc-lamps along boulevards; that last white rocket that went flaming across the sky, was the faery taxi which is to speed him on his happy errand. It isn't so, one has only to remember.

We were in the Somme for several months. The mud was up to our knees almost all the time. We were perishingly cold and very rarely dry. There was no natural cover. When we went up forward to observe, we would stand in water to our knees for twenty-four hours rather than go into the dug-outs; they were so full of vermin and battened flies. Wounded and strayed men often drowned on their journey back from the front-line. Many of the dead never got buried; lives couldn't be risked in carrying them out. We were so weary that the sight of those who rested for ever, only stirred in us a quiet envy. Our emotions were too exhausted for hatred—they usually are, unless some new Hunnishness has roused them. When we're having a bad time, we glance across No Man's Land and say, "Poor old Fritzie, he's getting the worst of it." That thought helps.

An attack is a relaxation from the interminable monotony. It means that we shall exchange the old mud, in which we have been living, for new mud which may be better. Months of work and preparation have led up to it; then one morning at dawn, in an intense silence we wait with our eyes glued on our watches for the exact second which is zero hour. All of a sudden our guns open up, joyously as a peal of bells. It's like Judgment Day. A wild excitement quickens the heart. Every privation was worth this moment. You wonder where you'll be by night-fall — over there, in the Hun support trenches, or in a green world which you used to sing about on Sundays. You don't much care, so long as you've completed your job. "We're well away," you laugh to the chap next you. The show has commenced.

When you have given people every reason you can think of which explains the spirit of our men, they still shake their heads in a bewildered manner, murmuring, "I don't know how you stand it." I'm going to make one last attempt at explanation.

We stick it out by believing that we're in the right — to believe you're in the right makes a lot of difference. You glance across No Man's Land and say, "Those blighters are wrong; I'm right." If you believe that with all the strength of your soul and mind, you can stand anything. To allow yourself to be beaten would be to own that you weren't.

To still hold that you're right in the face of armed assertions from the Hun that you're wrong, requires pride in your regiment, your division, your corps and, most of all, in your own integrity. No one who has not worn a uniform can understand what pride in a regiment can do for a man. For instance, in France every man wears his divisional patch, which marks him. He's jolly proud of his division and wouldn't consciously do anything to let it down. If he hears anything said to its credit, he treasures the saying up; it's as if he himself had been mentioned in despatches. It was rumoured this year that the night before an attack, a certain Imperial General called his battalion commanders together. When they were assembled, he said, "Gentlemen, I have called you together to tell you that tomorrow morning you will be confronted by one of the most difficult tasks that has ever been allotted to you; you will have to measure up to the traditions of the division on our left — the First Canadian Division, which is in my opinion the finest fighting division in France." I don't know whether the story is true or not. If the Imperial General didn't say it, he ought to have. But because I belong to the First Canadian Division, I believe the report true and set store by it. Every new man who joins our division hears that story. He feels that he, too, has got to be worthy of it. When he's tempted to get the "wind-up," he glances down at the patch on his arm. It means as much to him as a V. C.; so he steadies his nerves, squares his jaws and plays the man.

There's believing you're right. There's your sense of pride, and then there's something else, without which neither of the other two would help you. It seems a mad thing to say with reference to fighting men, but that other thing which enables you to meet sacrifice gladly is love. There's a song we sing in England, a great favourite which, when it has recounted all the things we need to make us good and happy, tops the list with these final requisites, "A little patience and a lot of love." We need the patience — that goes without saying; but it's the love that helps us to die gladly — love for our cause, our pals, our family, our country. Under the disguise of duty one has to do an awful lot of loving at the Front. One of the finest examples of the thing I'm driving at, happened comparatively recently.

In a recent attack the Hun set to work to knock out our artillery. He commenced with a heavy shelling of our batteries — this lasted for some hours. He followed it up by clapping down on them a gas-barrage. The gunners' only chance of protecting themselves from the deadly fumes was to wear their gas-helmets. All of a sudden, just as the gassing of our batteries was at its worst, all along our front-line S.O.S. rockets commenced to go up. Our infantry, if they weren't actually being attacked, were expecting a heavy Hun counter-attack, and were calling on us by the quickest means possible to help them.

Of a gun-detachment there are two men who cannot do their work accurately in gas-helmets — one of these is the layer and the other is the fuse-setter. If the infantry were to be saved, two men out of the detachment of each protecting gun must sacrifice themselves. Instantly, without waiting for orders, the fuse-setters and layers flung aside their helmets. Our guns opened up. The unmasked men lasted about twenty minutes; when they had been dragged out of the gun-pits choking or in convulsions, two more took their places without a second's hesitation. This went on for upwards of two hours. The reason given by the gunners for their splendid, calculated devotion to duty was that they weren't going to let their pals in the trenches down. You may call their heroism devotion to duty or anything you like; the motive that inspired it was love.

When men, having done their "bit" get safely home from the Front and have the chance to live among the old affections and enjoyments, the memory of the splendid sharing of the trenches calls them back. That memory blots out all the tragedy and squalor; they think of their willing comrades in sacrifice and cannot rest.

I was with a young officer who was probably the most wounded man who ever came out of France alive. He had lain for months in hospital between sandbags, never allowed to move, he was so fragile. He had had great shell-wounds in his legs and stomach; the artery behind his left ear had been all but severed. When he was at last well enough to be discharged, the doctors had warned him never to play golf or polo, or to take any violent form of exercise lest he should do himself a damage. He had returned to Canada for a rest and was back in London, trying to get sent over again to the Front.

We had just come out from the Alhambra. Whistles were being blown shrilly for taxis. London theatre-crowds were slipping cosily through the muffled darkness—a man and girl, always a man and a girl. They walked very closely; usually the girl was laughing. Suddenly the contrast flashed across my mind between this bubbling joy of living and the poignant silence of huddled forms beneath the same starlight, not a hundred miles away in No Man's Land. He must have been seeing the same vision and making the same contrast. He pulled on my arm. "I've got to go back."

"But you've done your 'bit,'" I expostulated. "If you do go back and don't get hit, you may burst a blood vessel or something, if what the doctors told you is true."

He halted me beneath an arc-light. I could see the earnestness in his face. "I feel about it this way," he said, "If I'm out there, I'm just one more. A lot of chaps out there are jolly tired; if I was there, I'd be able to give some chap a rest."

That was love; for a man, if he told the truth, would say, "I hate the Front." Yet most of us, if you ask us, "Do you want to go back?" would answer, "Yes, as fast as I can." Why? Partly because it's difficult to go back, and in difficulty lies a challenge; but mostly because we love the chaps. Not any particular chap, but all the fellows out there who are laughing and enduring.

Last time I met the most wounded man who ever came out of France alive, it was my turn to be in hospital. He came to visit me there, and told me that he'd been all through the Vimy racket and was again going back.

"But how did you manage to get into the game again?" I asked. "I thought the doctors wouldn't pass you."

He laughed slily. "I didn't ask the doctors. If you know the right people, these things can always be worked."

More than half of the bravery at the Front is due to our love of the folks we have left behind. We're proud of them; we want to give them reason to be proud of us. We want them to share our spirit, and we don't want to let them down. The finest reward I've had since I became a soldier was when my father, who'd come over from America to spend my ten days' leave with me in London, saw me off on my journey back to France. I recalled his despair when I had first enlisted, and compared it with what happened now. We were at the pier-gates, where we had to part. I said to him, "If you knew that I was going to die in the next month, would you rather I stayed or went?" "Much rather you went," he answered. Those words made me feel that I was the son of a soldier, even if he did wear mufti. One would have to play the game pretty low to let a father like that down.

When you come to consider it, a quitter is always a selfish man. It's selfishness that makes a man a coward or a deserter. If he's in a dangerous place and runs away, all he's doing is thinking of himself.

I've been supposed to be talking about God As We See Him. I don't know whether I have. As a matter of fact if you had asked me, when I was out there, whether there was any religion in the trenches, I should have replied, "Certainly not." Now that I've been out of the fighting for a while, I see that there is religion there; a religion which will dominate the world when the war is ended—the religion of heroism. It's a religion in which men don't pray much. With me, before I went to the Front, prayer was a habit. Out there I lost the habit; what one was doing seemed sufficient. I got the feeling that I might be meeting God at any moment, so I didn't need to be worrying Him all the time, hanging on to a spiritual telephone and feeling slighted if He didn't answer me directly I rang Him up. If God was really interested in me, He didn't need constant reminding. When He had a world to manage, it seemed best not to interrupt Him with frivolous petitions, but to put my prayers into my work. That's how we all feel out there.

God as we see Him! I couldn't have told you how I saw Him before I went to France. It's funny—you go away to the most damnable undertaking ever invented, and you come back cleaner in spirit. The one thing that redeems the horror is that it does make a man momentarily big enough to be in sympathy with his Creator—he gets such glimpses of Him in his fellows.

There was a time when I thought it was rather up to God to explain Himself to the creatures He had fashioned—since then I've acquired the point of view of a soldier. I've learnt discipline and my own total unimportance. In the Army discipline gets possession of your soul; you learn to suppress yourself, to obey implicitly, to think of others before yourself. You learn to jump at an order, to forsake your own convenience at any hour of the day or night, to go forward on the most lonely and dangerous errands without complaining. You learn to feel that there is only one thing that counts in life and only one thing you can make out of it—the spirit you have developed in encountering its difficulties. Your body is nothing; it can be smashed in a minute. How frail it is you never realise until you have seen men smashed. So you learn to tolerate the body, to despise Death and to place all your reliance on courage—which when it is found at its best is the power to endure for the sake of others.

When we think of God, we think of Him in just about the same way that a Tommy in the front-line thinks of Sir Douglas Haig. Heaven is a kind of General Headquarters. All that the Tommy in the front-line knows of an offensive is that orders have reached him, through the appointed authorities, that at zero hour he will climb out of his trench and go over the top to meet a reasonable chance of wounds and death. He doesn't say, "I don't know whether I will climb out. I never saw Sir Douglas Haig—there mayn't be any such person. I want to have a chat with him first. If I agree with him, after that I may go over the top—and, then again, I may not. We'll see about it."

Instead, he attributes to his Commander-in-Chief the same patriotism, love of duty, and courage which he himself tries to practice. He believes that if he and Sir Douglas Haig were to change places, Sir Douglas Haig would be quite as willing to sacrifice himself. He obeys; he doesn't question.

That's the way every Tommy and officer comes to think of God—as a Commander-in-Chief whom he has never seen, but whose orders he blindly carries out.

The religion of the trenches is not a religion which analyses God with impertinent speculation. It isn't a religion which takes up much of His time. It's a religion which teaches men to carry on stoutly and to say, "I've tried to do my bit as best I know how. I guess God knows it. If I 'go west' to-day, He'll remember that I played the game. So I guess He'll forget about my sins and take me to Himself."

That is the simple religion of the trenches as I have learnt it—a religion not without glory; to carry on as bravely as you know how, and to trust God without worrying Him.

THE END